Jesus Stories

apocryphile press
BERKELEY, CA

Apocryphile Press
1700 Shattuck Ave #81
Berkeley, CA 94709
www.apocryphile.org

ISBN 9781940671918
eISBN 9781940671925 (Kindle)
eISBN 9781940671932 (Epub)

Jesus
Stories

John R. Mabry

Table of Contents

Introduction

Have you ever wanted to hang out with Mary and Joseph, or Jesus and the disciples? What would it have been like to be a fly on the wall, or hiding unnoticed in a corner as some of the most familiar and beloved scenes played out? The Gospel accounts are so compact, I thought it would be fun to experience them as more immersive, fleshed-out narratives.

I have always loved stories about Jesus, especially those that add to the biblical accounts—I like the little details and even the significant departures from the "accepted" versions. I guess that's why I am "the Apocryphile" and have always loved apocryphal literature. So I decided to write some of my own. I consider these stories to be examples of "Gospel midrash," and I think you could make a good case for that!

Another way to look at them is as written examples of Ignatian prayer—I put myself in the Gospel stories, and then wrote down what I saw—the smells, the conversations, the surprises. It's a kind of Shamanic journey, guided by the broad outlines of the story. And as Shamanic journeys and Ignatian prayer experiences often are, they were frequently enlightening for me.

Most of the stories in this collection were originally written and delivered as sermons. I like to think that whenever I began a "narrative" sermon, my congregation was delighted. There is no objective evidence of this, because no one ever said a thing about them, strangely! But I always enjoyed the departure from "regular" sermonizing.

The most unusual of the pieces is the last one, "The Last Testament of Thomas." This one was not written as a sermon, but as a one-person play. This was the second draft, which was *way* too long for performance. My advisor said, "You've written a fine novella, but it's not a play." So I rewrote the play, but I let the novella stand in the form you see here.

It was born of my love of the literature of the Thomas school of early Christianity. For more on this and the theology of the Thomas school, please see my book *The Way of Thomas*. The stories in this novella are mostly drawn from the Thomas literature, specifically from the Gospel of Thomas, the Book of Thomas the Contender, and the Acts of Thomas. Although the Infancy Gospel of Thomas is not a product of the Thomas school, I have drawn stories from it in order to fill in the early portion of Jesus' life. And since Thomas' name is on the book, I figured I'd give myself a pass on that. You don't mind, do you?

It is probably tempting to try to read through these stories as if they were a novel, but that will result in some dissonance, as they were not written that way. Although they are arranged in chronological order, the depictions of Jesus are markedly different. The uncertain, bumbling Jesus of "The Wedding at Cana" has little in common with the surefooted Jesus of "A Resurrection," and almost nothing in common with the complicated Jesus of "The Last Testament of Thomas."

Nevertheless, I hope you will take each story for what it is, and enjoy the collection. These were each a joy to write, and I hope they will bring you some joy as well.

John R. Mabry
Oakland, CA
Advent 2015

Just a Baby

It was just a baby.

Just another sticky organ
mewling its independence.

It was just a baby.
It was nothing special.

Just another locus of divinity
in meat clothing.
A pearl cast into the dark, moist earth.

It was just a baby.
It was nothing special.

Except that someone told
his mother that
he *was*.

Joseph's Dream

Joseph had almost made it back to the woodshop when one of the children spotted him. Even though he knew Malachi would be waiting for him, he couldn't resist engaging them. He could hear them call his name from over the garden wall, and when he rounded the corner, there was not a single one of them in sight. He slung his bag of tools onto the other shoulder, and spoke, as if to himself, but loud enough that all of the children could hear, wherever they were hiding. "I thought I heard someone calling me! How strange, there's no one here!" He ignored the smallest of the children, who were, despite their best efforts, really in plain sight. He actually caught the eye of Tamar, and winked at her—she pulled a sack down over her eyes and tried to hold still. "Perhaps it was the Lord calling me, hm? The Lord has a much higher voice than I expected! Perhaps the Lord is a child, hm?"

He wanted to find Zeke's twins, since they had played a joke on him the other day, swapping out his iron nails with clay replicas they had rolled out themselves. It was a very funny joke, he had to admit, since he hadn't spotted the fake nails until he was already on the job site. Unfortunately, the customer had not been so amused when Joseph told him he would have to delay starting on the job to retrieve some more "supplies" from the shop. He stalked about the garden, wondering where he himself would have hidden at that age. Then he saw where a large spray of flowers created a curtain, and edged in that direction, but not too obviously. He crisscrossed the garden, always talking loudly to himself.

"And why should the Lord not talk to me, hm? If the Lord is hiding, I will find him!" At that, he tore aside the curtain of foliage to reveal a teenage couple in passionate embrace. The girl shrieked at their exposure, and ran away. The boy turned red and stammered incoherently. Joseph himself stammered a bit, "Oh, 1…look, I'm so sorry. I was looking for…someone else." The boy took advantage of his befuddlement and took off himself. Joseph felt a moment of heaviness come over him. The last thing he wanted to do was to discourage young lovers; he was too much in love himself. He felt ashamed for intruding on the couple, and sat down by the canopy of flowers.

And that was when he heard the giggles coming from above. He cocked his head to listen, but restrained himself from actually looking at the roof of the nearby house. "It's too bad I could not find those children," he said, too loudly, so that they all could hear. "I had a new toy to give them…I guess I'll just sell it in the shop instead."

At this he heard an excited rustle coming from the roof of the house, then a yelp. Before he could get up a boy of about eight fell in a heap near his feet. "OW!" the boy cried, and then groaned under his breath. It was Michael, one of Zeke's twins.

"Good thing we Jews build our houses so low to the ground, hm?" Joseph reached down and helped the child to his feet. He dusted him off and turned him around to make sure there was no permanent damage. "Now, where is your brother? I swear, there's nothing worse than twins."

Thomas called to him from the roof, "You said you had toys!"

"Come down from there and ask me politely!" Joseph spoke to the roof. He mussed Michael's hair and took a bear he had carved at lunch out of his sack. "I only have the one, so share this with your brother, okay?" At that all the smaller children "revealed" themselves, uncovering their eyes so that Joseph could see them.

"I can't carve toys all day!" he told them as they gathered around him. "But here," he passed a Roman coin to the eldest of the girls. "Make sure everyone gets a treat, okay?" And then they were all off in a herd toward the baker's shop.

He sat back down and enjoyed the sun on his face for a moment, but his reverie passed quickly. "Joseph!" It was Malachi's voice, and he did not sound happy. "I swear, man, if you weren't such a miracle worker, I would have fired you ages ago. I was expecting you before the third hour was up."

"You know how Benjamin and his wife can be," Joseph explained, "They have to talk through every last detail, even if there's nothing to fix." Malachi stared at him for a good long moment. "Well, that's true." Joseph was surprised to see that his expression was more worried than angry.

Malachi sat beside him near the canopy of flowers. "Your intended's mother is waiting for you in the shop," he said quietly. "If I were you, I'd just kill myself now, because if the Pharaoh had looked half as threatening when Moses came to see him as your mother-in-law looks now, we'd still be slaves in Egypt."

Joseph found that hard to believe. Anna was such a gentle woman, and she loved him. As long as he had been courting Miriam, both Anna and Joachim had treated him as their own son, with kindness, respect, and even a little awe. Malachi stood and stomped about nervously. "Look, I'm going to go home for a bit of a nap, okay? I'll give you two some privacy. I'll be back at the ninth hour, and we'll pour some hinges, yes?" Joseph nodded and waved a goodbye. Feeling older than he actually was, he swung the tool bag onto his shoulder once again and headed for the workshop.

***   ***   ***

"Anna?" he called, rounding the corner into the shop. He set his bag down on the waist-high planing bench and blinked, his eyes adjusting to the dim light. "There you are." Anna's voice was thick with both anger and tears. She rose and strode towards him with sudden fury. "We trusted you!" She shoved him in the chest. He stumbled backwards, but she kept coming, shoving him again and again. "We *loved* you! You bastard! Why didn't you just kill her with your own hand and get it over with?" Her final shove came with a force he could not anticipate and he stumbled over a bench. He picked himself up quickly and caught at her hands.

Anna was a slight, frail woman, nearly half his own size, but she wrestled herself from his grip effortlessly and swung around, catching his face with a slap that he was sure could be heard for blocks. "You gentile dog! You just couldn't wait until next year, could you? You had to have your satisfaction—who cares if it cost my Miriam her life? And us our honor? I pray God will toss you to the flames of Gehenna!" She slapped at him again and again, but now he simply let her hit him. He was dazed and his cheeks stung more than they hurt.

But his lack of resistance only made her angrier. Her tears nearly blinding her, she cast her hand about for some weapon, and found the hilt of a mallet on the bench behind his head. She swung it up above her and brought it down hard, catching Joseph in the temple. He slumped to the floor and she beat at his chest with her fists until she got sick and retched on the floor. Then she staggered to the doorway and collapsed.

*** *** ***

When Joseph woke, he instantly wished again for oblivion. His head pounded and his chest felt like it had been run over by a herd of goats. He tried to sit up and winced. "No…no…lay back down, Jo. I don't feel like cleaning up any more vomit." Malachi was pressing a cold, wet cloth to his forehead. He smelled myrrh, and knew his boss had been applying ointment to his wounds. "What happened?" he asked finally.

"I was hoping you could tell me," Malachi said. "When I

got here, Anna was passed out cold by the door there, and you looked like you got the raw end of a fight with a couple of she-lions."

"Only one she-lion, but she was fierce enough. Ow...."

"What did she say to you? What provoked...this?"

"I haven't got a clue. She said, 'Why didn't you just kill her and get it over with?' Kill who?"

"Could she be talking about Miriam?"

"She must be. She said something about 'Couldn't I have waited another year....'" Joseph sat upright, oblivious to the pain. "Malachi! What if...."

The thought occurred to Malachi at the same time. "The only thing I could think of that would make Anna this mad, was if Miriam were to be found...well, with child."

"Oh, God."

"Shh...don't blaspheme. Let's think this through. If we're right...and Miriam is...pregnant.... Joseph, did you two...you know?"

"We kissed! We *did* kiss, but I swear upon my parents' memory...I never violated her...trust." He clutched at Malachi's shirt-front. "Promise me you'll say nothing, Malachi! They'll kill her!"

Malachi, who was normally gruff, impatient, even condescending to him, pried his fingers from his own shirt and held them in his hands. "Joseph, we don't even know the whole story. I will keep every confidence you need me to. I promise." Joseph relaxed, and his head swam with grief.

The penalty for conceiving a child out of wedlock was death by stoning. Officially, both parties could be stoned, but since it was harder to implicate the man, and most of them denied it, more often than not it was only the woman who was killed. It happened a couple of times a year in Nazareth, more than in other cities, as Nazareth was not esteemed as the most moral of places. Joseph avoided stonings, as he felt such events were cruel and ought to be carried out in private. But he had seen a few, and in his mind's eye he saw his beloved Miriam in the center of a circle of blood-crazed righteous folk, bent on exacting the justice demanded by the Law of Moses. No mere man could intervene.

"She must have been raped, Mal! She would never consent, she loves me!" He was weeping now, and his friend hovered over him with the cool cloth, shushing him and touching his hair with uncharacteristic tenderness. After a while, Joseph's sobbing subsided. Finally, he said, "What should I do, Mal? I have to save her."

"We must think this through very carefully." For a while they kept silence. Eventually, though, Malachi said, "There's no way you can marry her, now."

Joseph knew it was true. She had shamed him. Even though they were not officially wed yet, they were engaged, and he was no less a cuckold. Even if the deed had been done without her consent, Miriam was damaged, used, and not a fit bride for any man with an ounce of self-respect.

"I'll break off the engagement..." he said, not believing the words coming from his own mouth. "We'll tell people...we'll tell them that Miriam was so grief-stricken at the breakup that she went to live with distant relatives."

Malachi finally sat. "That could work. I have a kinsman in Tyre that might take her in for a price. He's kind, and won't ask too many questions."

Joseph felt a spark of hope. "She could tell people in Tyre that her husband died soon after the child was conceived."

Malachi nodded. "People will talk, of course, but then people always talk. I think it's for the best, Joseph. I'm so sorry this has happened to you, my friend. Talk to Miriam in the morning; now, sleep."

*** *** ***

Joseph slept, but not well. He woke several times in the night, his head filled with worry, and he obsessed over half-baked schemes that could never work in the light of day. He knew it was wise to rest, however, and he forced himself to remain still, even if sleep evaded him.

Near dawn, his pain lifted and hovered in the air above him, and he found himself at the large workbench near the oven with Malachi, pouring hinges. The molds were scattered across the table, and Joseph was coating them with fat, while Malachi worked the bellows to heat the iron. There was a third man at the bench, too, but Joseph could not see his face. He was also busy, methodically smashing each of the molds as soon as Joseph had greased them. There seemed to be an endless supply of molds, however, and none of the three men were interrupted in their industry for what seemed like some time.

After a while, however, the man smashing the molds spoke, and when he did, it sounded like the rushing of water. "I will smash every hinge you make."

"Then shall I make more?" Joseph asked him, without bothering to look at the face he knew he could not see.

"Better to rest."

But Joseph just kept going. Rubbing the cloth in fat, swiping the inside of the molds. But then the pain hovering above floated down and settled upon his head like a crown of fire. His grief overcame him suddenly and he lowered his head to the table and wept.

"She has not been with you..." the faceless man said matter-of-factly, but Joseph took it to be a question.

"I swear she has not!"

"Nor has she been with any man."

"Then how...?" In answer, the stranger smashed another mold.

"I will unmake every thought you have, and every plan you make shall end in dust." Then the man's face which could not be seen shone suddenly with the brightness of the sun. Malachi seemed oblivious, but Joseph shielded his eyes with both hands.

The voice of many waters continued. "The child is mine. The girl shall not be killed, nor shall you divorce her. Today you sought after children, and played at finding God. But I tell you truly, if you find children, you find God."

The glowing countenance receded, and then the man whose face he could not see fastened one side of the hinge to the tabernacle where the Torah was kept in their local synagogue. The other side he fixed to a door, and yet, inexplicably, the door *was* the village—he could see all the people of the village in that door. Everyone in Nazareth, the miller, the blacksmith, the rabbi, the prostitutes; they were all there. "It must be loose," the stranger said, "or it will not work." He swung the door open and shut, open and shut.

The man swung the door faster and faster, until it made a noise like the beating of wings, and above the din, the faceless stranger spoke again. "God saves, my son. And that is what you should call him."

"Call who?"

"The baby."

Joseph woke covered in sweat, the roaring of wings in his ears.

*** *** ***

It was barely the third hour when Joseph stood outside Joachim and Anna's house. He stood there for a long time, not only uncertain what to say, but, he admitted to himself, afraid to face Anna's wrath again. "God give me the proper words," he whispered and strode to the door with a confidence he did not feel. He knocked and waited for what seemed an eternity.

Finally, the door opened a crack, and Joachim's lined, aged face peeked out. His brow furrowed when he saw who it was. "Father Joachim," Joseph pleaded, "I do not know who has visited such evil upon us all…but I love Miriam, and I would never dishonor her or you in such a way." And then he lost it and cried for every dream of happiness with her he had ever had. The door swung open, and Joachim reached out and pulled him to his breast.

"I believe you," he said, and they wept together.

After several minutes, their tears began to slow, and they simply held one another in mutual grief. "I never thought you could do this, Jo," Joachim said, drying his eyes. "But Anna needs someone to blame. Please forgive her." Then he seemed to notice Joseph's face for the first time. "And I see you have much to forgive." He smiled a little weakly, until he caught a glimmer of a smile in Joseph as well. "You think you look bad, Joseph? You should see what your face did to my wife's fists!"

Joseph almost laughed at that. But then he remembered himself. "Where is Miriam?"

Joachim looked around warily. "Anna is at market; be quick. Miriam is in the sleeping room. Behave yourself." Joseph winced; Joachim had meant it as a jest, but given the circumstances, it stung.

*** *** ***

When he drew back the curtain, she was there, a thirteen-year-old girl, rocking back and forth, trying to comfort herself. She was wrapped in every blanket in the room, although it was not a particularly chilly morning. "Is that you, Jo?" She did not turn around.

"It's me." He walked to the far side of the room to face her, and sat on a low bench.

Then she saw his face, and knew what her mother had done. "Oh, Jo, I'm sorry...I'm *so* sorry!" She cried, and there were more tears for both of them. She choked a bit as she spoke. "I told them, Amma and Abba, I told them I have never...I didn't...I never would betray you...or them. But they don't believe me."

Neither do I, Joseph thought, *or do I?* He felt a confusing mixture of compassion and anger. They were so close, so close to all their dreams coming true. What possible temptation…? And he knew there was none. He knew Miriam like his own soul, had known her since she was a baby, since he was a boy, and none of this made any sense at all. He would have staked his life on her, and without a moment of fear. "No other man but you, Joseph, has ever touched my lips." Her eyes locked on his own and held on for dear life. "And no man has defiled me. I swear to you. I swear to—"

"Shhh…don't blaspheme. We need all the help we can get right now." He reached out and took her hand. "If no man has touched you, how did this happen, hm?"

"I don't know!" Her face was contorted with despair and confusion. Could someone have taken her in her sleep? Drugged her? Could she be protecting someone, perhaps even Joachim? He banished the thought.

"Just before I missed my moon, I had a dream," she said. "I don't know why I'm telling you this; it isn't going to help us any. But it was very strange and Amma and Abba won't listen to anything I say right now."

"Tell me," he whispered.

"There was a man with no face, and his voice sounded like a river. And he hammered a nail into my palm, and another in my foot. It held me down on a large piece of wood, larger than I have ever seen. Then, he did the same with my other hand and foot, but this he nailed to a huge box. Then I realized that I was not a girl at all, but a hinge on the tabernacle at the synagogue…."

Joseph's jaw dropped and he felt suddenly faint.

Miriam continued, remembering and distant. "But before he closed the door, he asked me if it was okay. I told him, 'This is what I am meant to do.' And he swung the door shut and I was just there, inside the tabernacle with all the birds."

He wanted to say, "There aren't any birds in the tabernacle," but he remembered that this was a dream. And he also knew that the faceless man she saw was the same who had visited him the night before.

She didn't expect a response from him. She did not expect him to believe her. "What will become of me, Joseph? Will you hand me over to be killed, or will you be merciful and send me away?" She looked up at him, pleading for her life.

"What else can I do, my love?" He leaned in and kissed her on the cheek. "I will do neither. Instead, I will marry you…if you'll have me. I will marry you this very day, if you are willing. And then we'll move to a village where they don't know how to count. How's that?"

She searched the lines and bruises of his face for some hint of mockery, of cruelty, but she found only love. Her sobs came forth parched, dry, as if she could not position her throat or mouth to do it properly, and she clung to him ferociously.

"The child's name is Y'Shua," Joseph told her.

She leaned back to see his face again. "What do you mean?" She meant to say, "How can you think of such a thing right now?" But it was too strange a thing for him to say. She looked at him wonderingly.

"His name is 'God will save,' is what he said. 'Y'shua,' Joshua, Jesus."

"Who said this?"

"The man with no face, in my dream, last night." Joseph smiled. "I'm going to talk to your father. I'm going to suggest we leave soon after lunchtime. It's all going to be okay. But I want you to rest, to relax." He kissed her on the head. "A hinge must be loose or it won't work, you know." She clung to him, breathed her relief into his shirt, and wondered at the strange life taking form within her.

The **Weight** of the **Word**

The sunshine hurt her eyes. It also irritated her. Inside she felt bleak, and the heat and cheer of the midday sun seemed to mock her. It should be raining. It should be cloudy. It should be cold. The fact that the landscape around her did not match the one within rose up in her throat like a bitter wine, like medicine, like vinegar and gall.

She didn't notice that her feet hurt. She didn't notice how dusty her shift had become. She didn't notice that her left big toe had been cut on a rough stone and was trailing drops of blood on the path behind her.

She stopped to catch her breath, and, looking up, was surprised to see her destination looming ahead of her on a large hill. Seeing it, her heart began pounding and fear coursed through her, making her feel sweaty and faint. She leaned against a tree for support as her mind raced.

She had come because she had panicked. She had found herself in shame, suddenly, through no fault of her own, and there was no one she could tell. She imagined telling her mother, and the prospect terrified her. At best, she would be out on the street. At worst, her mother would have contacted the authorities. She had seen a woman who was pregnant out of wedlock once, when she was very small. She saw the men take up stones and pelt her until her face was mangled and bloody and no longer recognizable as human. She was that woman, now, and she shuddered at the thought.

It had been about six months since the angel had come. She spat in the dirt at the thought of that night. She had been so innocent, so naive, so stupid. And now she was starting to show. Her mother had mentioned that her Aunt Elizabeth was pregnant, and that she might need some help. It was an offhand bit of news that Mary had clung to like a lifeline. She secured an escort to the south shore of the Sea of Galilee the very next day.

And now here was Aunt Elizabeth's country manor, shining like a jewel under the too-bright, too-cheery sun. Mary's face twisted up, but she fought the urge to tears. What hope did she have that Elizabeth would be any more understanding than her own mother? After all, Elizabeth and her husband Zachariah were the "successful" ones in the family. While everyone else scraped together meager livings, Zachariah was the chief priest of the shrine at Tiberias. If word of Mary's shame got out, it would be Elizabeth and Zachariah who would have the most to lose.

She almost turned around. But then she noticed movement on the great house's veranda. She saw the lithe form of her Aunt Elizabeth, great with child. She saw the older woman start to wave, then double over sharply, then collapse onto the porch.

Mary ran to the house, her fears and self-loathing forgotten for the moment. Breathlessly, she called out for a servant, and then helped as a small army of maids and footmen swarmed around the grand lady. Gently, they carried her inside and laid her on a daybed in the large, stuccoed hall. Mary gratefully accepted a pot of water and a cloth from one of the maids and began to dab at Elizabeth's forehead. Her aunt had always doted on her, had given her far more encouragement then her own mother ever had. She had even nursed her when Mary had fallen ill as a young girl. It felt surreal to see their roles reversed now, and Mary felt the momentary reeling of vertigo.

But Elizabeth hadn't passed out, or not for long. Her eyelashes fluttered, and in a moment she focused on the young Mary's face. "Oh…" she said, her lips drawing back in a faint smile. "It's you."

"Yes, Auntie, it's me."

"You must be tired." Elizabeth's eyes flickered over the girl, taking her in.

Mary laughed involuntarily. "Don't you worry about me!" she said. "What happened to you? Are you sick? Are you all right?"

"It's the strangest thing…"

Mary continued to dab at her forehead with the cool cloth, noting for the first time how beautiful the creases in her Aunt's face were. She was old, she was weathered by this desert, certainly…and she was lovely. "Tell me," Mary insisted.

"I went out on the veranda, and the moment I saw you, he—" she indicated the enormous bulge that was her midsection—"he started kicking like a scared goat. I thought he was going to kick straight through me." She grimaced, trying to make light of it. "It's not like I'm not used to it, though."

"It's happened before?"

"Yes, last week. At the Simchat Torah celebration."

Mary nodded. That was the festival that celebrated the completion of the Torah. She loved that holiday, when the Torah scroll is taken from the synagogue, and the menfolk dance with it. The memory of it made her smile. "The moment the Torah scroll came into sight, he started kicking." Now Elizabeth smiled. "Zach says the baby's name will be John, but I want to name him Chamor."

Mary laughed loudly, then caught herself. *Chamor* was the Hebrew word for donkey. Elizabeth sat up. Mary began to protest, but the older woman held up her hand. "No, I'm fine. It passes quickly." She adjusted herself on the daybed and patted a spot beside her. She called for mint tea as Mary sat next to her and arranged her skirts modestly. "Now, child, I am very surprised to see you. Why are you here?" Her Aunt's face was kindly, but there was a serious edge to it that would tolerate no guile. Mary looked away, and her eyes began to fill with tears. Elizabeth reached out and touched her hand, but Mary still could not look at her. A servant carried in a tray with tea, and Elizabeth waved her and everyone else from the room. When they were alone, she said firmly, "Tell me."

Mary nodded and squeezed her hand. "I'm…I'm in trouble."

Elizabeth withdrew her hand. Mary thought she heard a note of ice enter her aunt's voice when she said, "Do you mean trouble…with a man?"

Mary swallowed and wiped her nose on the back of her hand. "Yes…no…not exactly."

"What…exactly?"

Mary turned to face the window, her back to her aunt. "You wouldn't believe me if I told you. You'd think I was…you'd think I was mad….or a liar….or a fool." With this Mary looked at the hands in her lap, shaking.

Elizabeth moved to put her arms around Mary, her head over her niece's shoulder, so that they both faced the window, still too bright. "Mary," she breathed softly. "Whatever you are afraid of won't stand a chance, not against the two of us." She squeezed, and Mary burst into tears.

When the sobs subsided, Mary turned to face her aunt again. "A man came to me. Except…except he wasn't a man."

Elizabeth cocked her head, trying to follow. Mary pounded her fist into the cushion. "You won't believe me!"

"Trust me, Mary, and I'll trust you. If it wasn't a man who came to you…but it *seemed* like a man, yes?" Mary nodded. "Did he have a name?" Mary nodded. "Was it *Gabriel*?"

Mary's head snapped up in shock, her face a mask of disbelief. "Ah…I see that it was," Elizabeth smiled, real mirth emitting from her crinkled eyes. "He has been a very *busy* angel, it seems."

"You *believe* me?" Mary breathed.

"Oh, yes, my dear," Elizabeth played with a lock of her niece's hair. "I haven't told anyone this…" she lowered her voice conspiratorially, "because I didn't think anyone would believe *me*."

"Tell me!" said Mary, a little too eagerly.

"Zach was making an offering at the shrine, you know, his big moment of the year. When he entered the tent of presence, he wasn't alone. There was a man, there." She smiled. "I think you know the one." Mary nodded as Elizabeth continued. "The man said that I'd bear a son, old as I am!" Her eyes looked wistful. "It's what we've always prayed for. The angel also said that he would be a great prophet—we're supposed to call him 'John,' a 'gift from God.'"

"What happened then?" Mary asked breathlessly.

"Oh, you know Zachariah. He couldn't just say, 'Yes, sir. Thank you, sir,' he had a thousand questions. He annoyed the angel so much that he struck him dumb." A pained look crossed her face. "Can't say as I blame him."

"Dumb? Zachariah can't speak? I can't imagine it!" Her uncle was always a man who loved to hear himself talk, after all.

"He came out of the tent of presence waving his arms like a madman, or like a child at some Purim guessing game!" Elizabeth laughed in spite of herself. "I have a feeling it isn't permanent," she said, as much to reassure herself as anything else. "When he can speak again, I'm hoping he'll be a wiser man."

Mary stared at the wall as if it wasn't there, and when she spoke, her voice had a far away sound to it. "He told me—the angel told me I would have a child, too." Her eyes met her Aunt's searchingly. "I didn't…I haven't. Joseph…I wouldn't betray him."

Elizabeth squeezed her shoulder. "A year ago, you would have been right. I *wouldn't* have believed you. But now…I wonder, does Joseph know?"

Mary nodded. "But I didn't tell him."

"The angel came to him, too?"

She shook her head. "Not in the same way. He had a dream."

Elizabeth rose suddenly and paced the room, holding onto

the child in her belly. "That's the way it happens, I suppose. I had a dream, too. I was kind of expecting you."

"You were?" Mary asked, her wonder becoming almost more than she could bear.

"Yes. I dreamed that we gave birth together, and that my son and your son were born as a single being, back-to-back. Then, suddenly, they were all grown up. They were still connected. My son was looking backwards, into the past, preaching to our ancestors, to Abraham and David and Elijah and Isaiah. Your son was facing the other way, of course, looking forwards, into the future, preaching to other people, but…I didn't know who they were—some were of our own people, but some were Gentiles, too." She stared off into the distance, remembering it, her face ghostly and pale. "But the most horrible thing was that my son's head was severed, and he held it under his arm as he preached, and your son bled from all his members. But still they preached and preached. They were still preaching when I woke up." She turned and faced Mary. "It was horrible."

Mary felt as if an icy blade twisted in her stomach. "What did you say?" Elizabeth asked her. "What did you say to the angel when he told you about your child?"

"I said…*yes*," Mary's lip quivered.

"Maybe you *are* a fool," Elizabeth said, half-mockingly. "You and my husband both."

"I'm scared," Mary said.

"Now that, I think, is wise." Elizabeth stepped over to her and took her hands.

"God turns everything upside down," Mary said, "I don't understand it, and I don't want it."

"You can say 'no,' anytime," Elizabeth told her. "I know midwives who can make the whole scary situation go away, if that's what you want. Or you stay here until the baby comes—we'll tell your mother I need you to nurse me—and then give the child to another old couple like me and Zach, who will be grateful for him, and raise him well, and you can go back to your mother with her none the wiser."

Mary searched her face for a clue that she was kidding. Here was hope, freedom, a solution. "Or..." Elizabeth added. "You can say yes today, too. And tomorrow, you'll have to choose again. Every day you will have to choose whether you will say yes to God or not—we all do."

Mary sat down again, nodding, her heart beating fast, her throat thick with tears and possibility.

"And even if you choose to say 'yes' everyday, you can still stay here until the baby comes. I really *could* use your help." Then she started to say something, but caught herself.

"What?" Mary asked.

"If you really want to do this. If you really want to go through with this. If you really want Joseph to make an honest woman of you...why not send for him, and let Zach marry you here. We'll have a quiet wedding." Elizabeth smiled. "And if Zach's still not speaking, it will be *very* quiet indeed!"

Mary laughed at this, but in the end, that is what they did. Joseph came, and Zachariah said the ancient words silently, for the ears of God alone. Mary and Joseph made their vows, and a clay pot broke beneath the heel of Joseph's sandal. It seemed strangely fitting to Mary while it was happening, this silent wedding. The air seemed too thin and delicate to support words of such great import, and the Word that grew within her seemed very heavy indeed.

A Prophet in Israel

Joshua's face hardened with resolve, and he drew himself up to his full, yet still diminutive height, and assumed an imperious air that would have befit a prince, a prophet, or even a judge. But as Joshua was none of those things, Mordecai laughed at him. The older, darker man punched at Isaac, their companion and, feigning an aside, said, "Look at him, swollen up like a rotting bladder in the sun. I need a pin. Do you have a pin, Isaac?"

Joshua wasn't budging. It would take more than teasing to sway him. He planted his hands on his hips and stamped his foot. "We can't stop here," he said again. "There's no tree shelter for the sheep. What if it rains?"

Mordecai was just as stubborn. "It's *not* going to rain. I want to sleep under the stars."

Isaac rolled his eyes at yet another standoff between his fellow shepherds. Timorously, he offered an olive branch. "Joshua, do you *have* to pick another fight?"

"I'm not picking a fight! Do you think I want to fight?" Joshua's tone was hurt. "That's the last thing I want. I have to speak up, though. Otherwise who will speak for the sheep?"

Just then a loud bleating filled the air, and Mordecai laughed. "You see? They don't need you. Look, little Moses, let's meet halfway, shall we? Let's make camp here—it's closer to the trees, but it still has a little hillock we can lay on, to enjoy the sky."

Joshua looked at where he was pointing. The tree cover wasn't nearly as dense, which he didn't like. But, on the other hand, the hillock was much lower. It was a true compromise, he realized, and reluctantly, he nodded.

"Bless God!" Mordecai exclaimed. "The lad *can* see sense."

Within moments they had driven the sheep to the spot Mordecai had indicated, and Isaac set about making a fire at the crown of the hillock.

Soon the little flame became strong, and leapt in a cheery and lively manner, creating a play of dancing shadows on the shepherd's faces. Joshua opened a worn cloth bag and took out a large, dark hunk of bread about twice the size of his fists. Mordecai and Isaac did the same. Mordecai surprised them by also pulling a wedge of cheese out of his own bag, but as he did not offer to share it, the younger men pretended not to notice.

Not to be outdone, Joshua drew a small clay jar from his bag, and slowly, deliberately broke the wax seal. He could feel the other men's eyes upon him as he did so, and he took his time, tormenting them. Tipping the pot, he poured a viscous stream of olive oil onto his bread. Carefully he set the pot down and bit into his meal with an exaggerated display of ecstasy playing out upon his face.

"You *are* going to share that, right?" Mordecai said, hopefully.

"My mother packed it as a surprise," Joshua said, not answering the question. "The first fruit from the new orchard."

He took another languorous bite and emitted a tiny "mmmm" of satisfaction. Isaac rolled his eyes again and turned away from his companions, preferring the stillness of the descending night.

After dinner, the men spread out their blankets and stared up at the stars. Joshua didn't dare say it out loud, but he hated being so out in the open, so vulnerable. He was concerned that the sheep have the cover of trees, but the truth was, he craved it himself. But he wasn't going to let Mordecai know that.

"They've finished the new Roman garrison," Isaac broke the stillness. "I've never seen anything like it. Sol says it's a Persian-style building. It's impressive, I'll tell you that."

Joshua chewed on a piece of grass. "What's he waiting for?"

"What's who waiting for?" Isaac asked.

"God. What's he waiting for? The Romans are raping this land, oppressing our people—God's people. I understand why we should suffer for our sins, but enough is enough. Why is there no prophet in Israel speaking out? What is the Holy One waiting for?"

"Maybe he's sleeping," Mordecai offered grumpily. "I know it sounds good to me."

"Blasphemer," Joshua accused.

"You wish. Then you could stone me." Mordecai slapped at his arm. "You'd love that, wouldn't you, Little Moses?"

Joshua fumed quietly. Mordecai had that mix of arrogance and bitterness you found in men who had failed at everything *except* shepherding. For Joshua and Isaac, it was a stepping stone to greater responsibility, but for Mordecai it was the end of the line, and he was going to make them pay for it. Every day, apparently.

"God's not sleeping," Joshua said, as if saying it like he believed it would make it so. Under his breath, he added, "But I'd sure like to see some evidence of that."

Just then a slow rumbling began. It was faint at first, as if from far away. The sheep began to bleat in a wild cacophony. The rumbling came closer, and the hillock to which they clung began to buck beneath them.

"What in the name of—" Mordecai began, suddenly wide awake.

Joshua sat up and drew his blanket tighter about him. His mouth dropped open and he pointed to the sky in the East. The other two men followed his gaze and gasped. Across the sky a shimmering curtain of color was hung. Regal purples, shining whites, and stark crimsons, the colors melted into each other and shone brighter than the moon.

"Blessed are you..." Mordecai began, but Joshua shushed him.

"Don't blaspheme, not now…"

And as Joshua stared at the sky, a stranger strode up to them out of the darkness and squatted by their fire.

Joshua barely gave him a glance. Travelers were common, and the shepherds often shared their fire with someone they encountered in the fields. But what seemed strange was that the man seemed oblivious to what was happening in the sky. "Mister, can't you see this?"

"Oh, yes. It's lovely, isn't it? One of my favorites."

Something about the stranger's tone unnerved Joshua. He focused his gaze upon him. He wasn't dressed like a traveler. In fact, it wasn't clear that he was dressed at all. Whenever Joshua tried to focus on the man's tunic, his focus shifted and shimmered like the curtain of light blazing across the sky.

Casually, the man reached for Mordecai's food bag and rummaged around. With a grin of satisfaction, he pulled out what was left of the cheese and popped it into his mouth. "I love cheese," he told Joshua.

Joshua looked at Mordecai wondering why the gruff, older man wasn't taking the stranger's head off for stealing his cheese.

The stranger clucked. "He can't see me. I came to speak to you."

Joshua's jaw dropped for the second time that evening. "You're—you're a—"

"Yes," the man grinned, rummaging deeper into the bag. "I'm a messenger."

"Wha—what are you doing here?" Joshua managed.

"What do you think? Bringing a message."

"To who?"

The man looked at Joshua as if the young shepherd were dim. "To you, silly."

Joshua sat frozen, not knowing what to say.

"Don't you want to know?" the messenger asked.

"What? Don't I want to know…what?"

"What the message is, of course." The messenger looked more and more dubious about the target of his mission.

"W—yes, of course I do."

"Then listen well. The Lord of Hosts saith unto thee: I am not asleep."

"I d—I didn't think he was."

"I'm not finished. Please don't interrupt a messenger. We're not allowed to write these things down and they're often long and convoluted."

"I'm sorry," Joshua said anxiously. "Please go on."

"Where was I? Oh, yeah, the Lord of Hosts says: I am not asleep. In fact I am…I am…. Poop. I lost it. Well, it wasn't complicated. I'll just give you the gist. God is coming to save his people. In fact, he's coming *tonight*."

Without another word, the messenger reached for Joshua's food. Opening the bag he emerged with the pot of olive oil. Removing the cork, he placed his finger in the oil and said a blessing in Hebrew. Then he replaced the cork and smiled at Joshua. "Don't be afraid, this is good news for everybody. There *is* a prophet in Israel, Joshua. He was born this very night, just a couple of hours ago. He is the anointed one, who will bring salvation to all peoples."

"I *knew* it…" Joshua breathed. "God did not abandon us."

"Pish, you *are* a silly one," the messenger said, brushing the dust from his rump. "Go to him," the messenger said. "Tonight. Take this," he handed Joshua his own bag of food.

"Where? Where will I find him?" Joshua asked, breathless.

"Oh…I don't know…" the messenger cocked his head and smiled at him. "Look for a spot that sheep would like."

The moon was glowing bright as Joshua and Mordecai picked their way through the outskirts of Bethlehem. Joshua had been an idiot, of course. He told Mordecai and Isaac what he had seen, and he had been sorry ever since. Isaac chalked it up to a hallucination inspired by the strange lights in the heavens, and offered to stay with the sheep.

Mordecai, of course, could not pass up a chance to tease Joshua without mercy for such craziness, and wouldn't have missed their night journey for the world.

"A messenger, you say? Did he have wings, then? I've always wondered what color their wings were. Did he have feathers, or are they skin wings, like a bat?"

Joshua ignored him, and continued in the vague direction the messenger had been looking as he spoke about the new prophet. And then he saw it—a lush meadow just within sight of the city. He stood in the middle of it and waited. He didn't see anyone.

"I don't see any prophets," Mordecai said, "not even little ones."

Joshua ignored him and bounced up and down on the balls of his feet, charged with excitement and confusion.

"We could start looking under rocks," Mordecai offered unhelpfully.

Just then Joshua felt a drop of rain on his face. He turned to Mordecai with a mild air of triumph. "Told you."

"You get to be right about one thing tonight, I guess," Mordecai conceded.

Where would sheep most like to be? He asked himself. And then he saw it. Barely noticeable in the moonlight, the mouth of a cave was discernible against the rocky hills to his right.

Without a word, Joshua strode off towards it, leaving Mordecai little choice but to follow.

Joshua paused at the lip of the cave, but he could see the light of a candle deep within. Relieved, he went in.

He wasn't sure what he had expected, but it wasn't this. He had expected priests and temple-style rituals to attend the birth of a prophet. At least a goat sacrifice, something. But there weren't any priests. And the goats, of which there were many, were very much alive. The cave was warm with them, and overwhelmingly fragrant as well.

And there, crouched over the feeding trough, was a peasant. Beside him, a woman slept. As Joshua approached, the man looked up with alarm.

"It's okay," Joshua spoke calmly. "We're friends. We're…shepherds."

Comprehension resolved the panic in the peasant's face, and he nodded. "It's a cold night. Is it raining?"

"Yes, it's just starting."

"Well, come in—are there two of you? I don't think there's room for your sheep, but you can certainly stay warm and dry with us."

The woman stirred, and the peasant fellow shushed her. Ignoring him, she opened her eyes and turned over facing them with a fierce look. Her husband whispered to her, and she relaxed.

"We don't have a fire," she said apologetically.

"We have goats. They're very warm," the peasant fellow smiled.

"We didn't come here to get warm, or to stay dry," Joshua said. He noticed the peasant man stiffen again. "No, it's okay, we haven't come to rob you, or to hurt you. I saw a messenger…."

The man looked at his wife, and then they both studied the young man with greater interest.

"Ah, he *says* he saw a messenger," Mordecai clarified. "I don't see things. I'm the sensible one. I'd be very glad to enjoy your hospitality."

But the young couple ignored him. They were fixed on Joshua. "Tell me about him," the peasant man asked.

"Well, he was very friendly, very relaxed. He wore—well, it's hard to describe what he wore." Joshua screwed up his face, frustrated at the difficulty. "But he told me that a prophet was born tonight in Israel. The anointed one." Joshua shyly walked towards them. He knelt by the trough. "Is this him?"

Pulling away the straw, Joshua saw the baby sleeping. He saw him squirm, swallow, and bite at his tiny hand.

His heart was moved, but he sighed, slightly disappointed. "He's not what I expected," he confessed.

"What do you mean?" the woman asked him.

"The messenger said he would be anointed. I expected to find a priest or a prophet here, I mean...to anoint him. You know, some kind of ceremony. There's nothing holy about...well, he's just a baby."

The woman caught her husband's eye and her lip curled into the slightest of smiles.

"Yes, he's just a baby," the man said with finality. "But who's to say God didn't send a prophet to anoint him?"

"What? Who—you mean Mordecai?" But Mordecai was already curled up in a circle of goats, seemingly oblivious to their conversation.

"No, I mean you."

"He's no prophet," a protest arose from the dormant pile that was Mordecai. "He preaches to sheep."

"I care about my sheep!" Joshua called in Mordecai's direction.

"Well, that's what a prophet does," said the man with quiet assurance. "He cares about his sheep."

Joshua puzzled about this for a moment, but then felt a cold chill run down his spine. "The messenger told me where to find you," he told the couple. "But he also blessed this." He drew the tiny pot from his bag.

"What is that?" the woman asked.

"I'm going to guess that's oil," her husband smiled knowingly. Joshua nodded and held the pot like it were a live animal, perhaps a scorpion.

"Go ahead," the woman said. "It's why the messenger sent you."

"But I'm no prophet. I'm a shepherd."

"So was David, and he was anointed king," the man reminded him. "Even the Lord is a shepherd sometimes."

Joshua remembered David's Psalm. It was true. With trembling fingers, he popped the cork from the jar, and dipped in a finger. Willing his hand steady, he moved toward the baby and touched his finger to his forehead. "I anoint you prophet over Israel," he said as he did it. He didn't know where the words were coming from. He just let them come. "And you will bring salvation to all people."

His finger lingered on the child, feeling the warmth of it, the holiness, the wonder.

The moment passed, and he sat down on the straw on the other side of the trough from the young couple. The woman looked at him with soft and tender eyes. Neither of them seemed the slightest bit surprised by any of this.

As they strode back toward their sheep, Joshua was lost in thought.

"Don't know why we couldn't have stayed until morning," Mordecai complained. "But at least it isn't raining any more."

"God wasn't sleeping," Joshua thought out loud, "I was." He stopped short.

"What? What are you stopping for?" Mordecai complained.

"That little baby won't be a prophet in Israel for another twenty years or more."

"Yeah, so?"

"So, until he's ready, who is going to speak for God? Someone has to be out there."

"What, you? What makes you think God would speak to you?"

"He did tonight," Joshua breathed. Mordecai said not a word. Joshua had been right about everything, after all, right down to the smallest detail.

Without another word, Joshua turned on his heel and began walking briskly back the way they had come.

"Where are you going?" Mordecai implored.

"Back to the cave. There's still some of that oil left, and someone has to anoint *me*."

A Light to Enlighten the Gentiles

The Persians were only a half-day's ride short of Jerusalem when the bandits hit them. A rock shot out of the pre-dawn curtain of rose light and nicked Balthazar just above the temple. He let out a cry, blacked out, and rolled off his camel, dropping nine feet to the sand like a rag doll. Caspar hurried to him to see what was wrong, nearly leaping off of his own mount, but Melchior drew his sword and sniffed the wind. He heard them before he saw them. They were quiet, he had to give them that, but the rattle of weapons gave them away as they walk-ran towards them from the still-dark West.

Melchior turned his camel around to meet them and charged, leaning from his seat to draw the blood of the first man he met. The bandits were not expecting retaliation, and the point man among them was not expecting the shadowy silhouette to move toward them, certainly not swinging a long, curved Babylonian blade. By the time he realized the Persian was a threat, Melchior was upon him. The blade swung up, and carved the bandit's neck straight up through his ears. Melchior swung down and blocked the path to his fallen comrade with a two-handed stance that left no doubt about his intentions or ability. The blood of the point bandit was gathering in a black pool barely visible in the dim light, but everyone could smell it. It made the camels even more nervous than the sudden excitement, and for a moment, it seemed the world was frozen as the remaining bandits squared off to size up their unexpectedly dangerous prey.

In the end, they were simply too many for him. A thick scarf fell from the face of one of the bandits, and Melchior could easily see that the man was an Israelite. No surprise there, given the neighborhood, but Melchior was shocked to see that the man bore a royal crest on his vestment. The bandit lunged, and as Melchior parried to meet his thrust, another bandit came from his other side and struck the back of his head with the flat of his blade. Melchior, too, dropped to the sand. The bandits took him by the arms and dragged him to where the other two Persians lay in the sand. One of them went to gather the two camels, now riderless, and brought them back to the others. His fellows lost no time emptying their packs in search of booty.

Caspar's eyes narrowed as he took in his attackers, and then widened in alarm as he recognized Melchior's body being dragged toward him. "Take what you want," he said to the tallest of the bandits. He, too, noticed the royal crest and wondered what it meant. "But I beg you to leave my companions alive. They have done you no wrong, and we throw ourselves upon the mercy of the God of Israel." It was a calculated formula, designed to strike fear into an Israelite. Caspar didn't believe a word of it. There was only one God in the universe, after all, and that was Ahura Mazda. But Caspar knew how Israelites thought, or at least how they *should* think according to his studies.

"State your business in Jerusalem," the leader spat.

"How do you know we're going to Jerusalem?"

"What? Do you think I'm an idiot? You're half a day's ride, and heading due west. If you're not heading to Jerusalem, you're going through it. State your business and do it quick or it will be my mercy you will be throwing yourselves on."

Caspar swallowed, and licked his parched lips. What to tell them? How much to tell them? Based on the royal crest on the man's clothes, he decided upon a strategy. "We are emissaries of his royal highness, Phraataces, the emperor of Persia and all its territories. We come directly from his court to seek an audience with the king of the Jews."

The man weighed what Caspar said carefully. The Persian could almost see his brains working. The travelers were not dressed in finery, but that was simply appropriate caution for traveling without the protection of an entourage. The man's speech, however, was fine, the camels in good shape, and the packs contained more treasure than the bandit had seen in more than a year. He nodded and told the Persian, "Then you are in luck. We are in the employ of the King of Judea, Herod, God's anointed." The man smiled. "We will take you to him."

The man's fellows were fastening the loot to their own packs. "Tell me," Caspar said through clenched teeth, "How shall we come to your king with no gift to offer? Shall we tell him that his soldiers have received it for him? For I can easily tell him that we bore twice or even thrice what you have taken."

The leader of the bandits smiled grimly. "We have gotten off on the wrong foot. We are a simple security patrol and mistook you for bandits—an easy assumption to make, is it not?" The leader could tell Caspar was not buying it. He sighed. "We will bear your gifts to the king directly, and you may tell him whatever you like." Balthazar was beginning to stir, and groaned loudly. Caspar smoothed his hair and whispered "Shhh..." over him, feeling a great wave of relief. Melchior, too, had begun to stir and was now glaring at their captors, clutching at the wet wound on his scalp.

"Get these men back on their camels," the tall man said to the other guards with a twinkle in his eye. "They are our honored guests, and we must make sure their gifts reach Herod safely."

*** *** ***

Joseph led the donkey east and tried to ignore his headache. The mid-afternoon sun was thankfully behind him, for the burning behind his eyes was bad enough. He put one foot in front of another and reminded himself that he had endured harder journeys. But he had gotten more sleep back then. The six days since the baby was born were a blur of negotiation, the screaming of little lungs, and the noxious smell of soiled swaddling clothes. His temper was wearing thin in the most obvious of places, and Mary was barely speaking to him. They had named the boy "Jesus," or "God saves," at Mary's insistence. "God save me from this child," Joseph breathed as he trudged onward. He didn't really feel that way, but he was tired, frustrated with his wife, and in a considerable amount of pain. In his short career as a father, it was not his best day.

"What?" Mary called ahead from the donkey. She was perched precariously, balancing the baby who was, at the moment, blessedly silent. "Did you say something?"

"Just reciting a prayer," he called back over his shoulder. "We will need to find shelter, soon." The traveling was excruciatingly slow. It should only have been a day's journey from Bethlehem to Jerusalem, but at this pace, Joseph could see it was going to take two. He knew there was an inn about midway between Bethlehem and the Holy City. They had not been lucky with inns of late, but Joseph held on to his hope.

He didn't really want to go to Jerusalem, and would have been content to do the circumcision in Bethlehem and then join a caravan north to Nazareth. But Mary had insisted that Jesus be circumcised by her uncle, the high priest Zachariah. Joseph had met the old man once, and while he was obviously cultured and intelligent, the young man felt slighted by his treatment. Joseph was just a carpenter after all, not a member of the intelligentsia. He was not a player in national politics, he was not rich, or a rabbi, or even particularly religious. In short, Joseph possessed nothing of value to the old man. So Zachariah had been *polite*, which, in Joseph's vocabulary, was another word for *insult*.

***   ***   ***

Herod was not at all pleased to have his morning toiletries inter-rupted by notice of the "emissaries" from Persia. Consequently, he made them wait until much later than his normal hour for hearing audiences. Balthazar was getting restless, for they knew their time was short, and he could not abide being caged, how-ever fancy the cage seemed to be. When Herod finally did call for them, it was nearly noon, and the tetrarch was already well-sopped with wine. The Persians bowed low and stayed that way until Herod spoke.

"I hear you bring me greetings from the noble Phraataces." Balthazar, as the official spokesperson, rose up and addressed the King. "Not really, your highness, no."

The tall man who had led the assault upon them looked as if he had been struck in the face by an impertinent concubine. "Oooo," cooed Herod. "This may be more interesting than I had anticipated."

"It is true, your highness, that we are in Phraataces' employ, and that we are courtiers of the emperor. He did not send us but we look forward to making known to him what we may discov-er."

"Out of favor, are we?" Herod grinned as he saw the redness rise in Balthazar's neck. "Well, far be it for me to upset your po-litical maneuvering."

"We were on our way to Jerusalem when we were set upon by thieves who attacked us without provocation and looted our saddlebags."

"Really?" He looked at the tall man standing at attention to his right. "That's not the story Agbar tells." His eyes twinkled as he spoke. "Could you not see my royal seal upon the tunics of my men?"

"Not in a pre-dawn ambush, sire, no, not clearly."

Herod made a pouty face. "I regret my lieutenant did not properly identify himself and his men, but he assures me that all of your belongings are here, and safe." He pointed to an ornate chest.

"I beg your highness' leave to select an appropriate gift before we depart. I wish we had been permitted to offer it upon greeting you."

Herod shifted in his seat, "Yes, your rudeness is hardly your fault. Now, tell me, what errand graces my court with your presence?"

"If it pleases your majesty, we are priests of the One God, Ahura Mazda, lord of the universe, whom you yourself worship in your temple here in Jerusalem." Herod noted with delight that this announcement had set his religious advisers to buzzing off to his left. This was more and more interesting, and he was no longer conscious of the effect of the wine or the normally troubling fact that he was not drinking more of it. "We have noted a new star in the West, and according to our calculations, such an appearance augers the birth of a new king. Due to its position in the sky, it was clear that this would be a king of the West. And Jerusalem is almost as far west as we can go. We came seeking news of the babe to carry to our lord, Phraataces. We hoped it would…please him."

"I'm sorry to disappoint you, but I have no child born recently, nor any on the way."

Balthazar looked confused. "That cannot be! Perhaps you have a wife who has not told you?"

Herod's eyebrows rose. "I'll check into that."

"P-p-perhaps your brother tetrarchs," Balthazar stammered.

"Not that I know of." Herod was enjoying toying with this priest. It would have been cruel if he had indeed known of such a child, but he was entirely ignorant of any princelings on the scene. No, this was entirely justifiable torture, and Herod was loving it.

The Zoroastrians huddled and whispered animatedly for a rather long time. They looked shaken, defeated, and uncertain as to how to proceed. After another burst of consultation, Herod interrupted them. "Care to share?" he asked impatiently.

"My lord," Balthazar said nervously, "we wonder if perhaps we are not simply witnessing the birth of a new king—indeed, such a sign as this has never been seen before, so it is possible we have ascribed its meaning to too mundane an event."

Herod was not sure whether that was an insulting comment or not, and his brow furrowed as he listened. "We wonder if perhaps it heralds a new *dynasty*."

Herod shot up out of his seat, sending wine cups and platters of sweetmeats scattering across the marbled floors. "Do you want to *die*, Persian?" Everyone's eyes were fixed upon the King except for the tangle of scribes and Pharisees arguing in the corner. One of them broke from the pack and bowed low to the king. "If it please your majesty, I would like to be heard."

Herod was just about to throttle Balthazar, and the Pharisee's intervention might indeed have saved him. "A little privacy, please, your majesty."

Herod's fingers shook in the air just about as high as Balthazar's throat, but the King allowed himself to be turned aside. "This had better be good," he told the Pharisee.

"Your majesty, we often speak of the King as God's anointed. But God anoints men for different reasons." He spoke the word for *anointed* not in Aramaic, but in Hebrew, *Meshiah*. "Perhaps this is the *messiah*, your majesty. Perhaps this is the one who will grow up to wield God's vengeance against Rome, a new Moses who will free our people once and for all!" The Pharisee's face was positively shining.

Herod hated religious people and resented the daily compromises he had to make with them to maintain his throne. He did not share the Pharisee's excitement, for he knew the people hated him. He ruled at Rome's pleasure, and if Rome were deposed, batty a notion as that actually was, he had no doubt that he and his would not be occupying any palaces. More likely they would be stoned, with no small amount of rejoicing to follow.

"And does the Torah tell us where such a one would be born, then?"

The Pharisee rushed back to the gaggle of black robes in their corner, and after a few moments of furious articulation, he shuffled back and whispered. "The Law does not tell us, your majesty, but the prophets do. He is to be born in Bethlehem, the city of David." His eyes were wild with promise.

The news came like a punch in the gut to Herod. Bethlehem was, after all, due west of Jerusalem. The Zoroastrians had been right. They had simply not gone far enough, and they surely would have, had his men not stopped them. His head swam as he weighed what to do. He felt behind him for his throne, and climbed into it uncertainly, shaking and pale. He was not up against any proper foe, now. He did not battle against flesh and blood, people who could be tortured, imprisoned, exiled or executed. He now opposed powers and principalities beyond his ability to manipulate. The Holy One of Israel was girding his loins to ride out against him, to put an end to his comfort and control. He trembled.

"My beloved princes and priests of Persia—" His tone was no longer condescending, but formal and measured, in inverse proportion to how out of control he was actually feeling. "—we have waited long for such a king. Go and greet him for us, but be sure you return to us when you have found him. For we have our own obeisance to make." His words were thick and dry. Forgotten were his wines and fruits and concubines and political machinations. They were the words of a man naked with terror, a man who has seen the hordes massed against him, with no hope of divine intervention. "And to ensure your speedy report," his eyes focused now, nearly running them through with their piercing intensity, "we will keep your treasure safe until you return."

The Zoroastrians glanced at one another, and bowed low, retreating backwards from the king's presence.

"Lieutenant," Herod called, waving the man to him. Agbar

approached the throne and leaned in as the king continued to motion him closer. "Take as many troops as you need," he whispered, "and make for Bethlehem this very day."

The soldier waited. He had an inkling what he was supposed to do when he got to Bethlehem, but he wanted to hear it from Herod's own lips. "Kill every male child in the city," he said, with a faraway look. "Kill. Every. One. Of. Them." He looked up into the soldier's eyes and focused for a moment. "Any questions?" The Lieutenant shook his head and grinned for all he was worth. This was going to be a *very* enjoyable mission. Never had bloodlust been so well rewarded. He was a man who *loved* his work.

*** *** ***

Balthazar tossed on his cot, his head swimming with relief and danger. He said a quick prayer to Good Mind and waited for his thoughts to quiet. Caspar and Melchior were taking their supper in the tavern affixed to the inn, but he was still nauseous from their ordeal, and the thought of food repulsed him.

They had not gone far from the throne room when one of the Pharisees rushed up to them excitedly and informed them of the prophecy regarding Bethlehem. They were exceedingly grateful for this revelation; it made a lot of sense. But their start was late indeed, and moving slow from their injuries, they had not gotten far that day. *Tomorrow*, he thought, *Bethlehem.*

After Herod's men had cleaned them out, they were frantic over what gifts they might still be able to offer the prince when they found him. Balthazar still had some gold coins, tied up tightly in a scarf bound around his waist. Beyond that, they were in a quandary. Caspar had a supply of medicinal myrrh in his travel apothecary. It wasn't much, but it was still valuable. Melchior, who normally served as a sacristan at home, came up with a bundle of frankincense from their liturgical supplies. All in all, it was a pretty meager offering, not at all proper for a royal audience, but he forced himself to dismiss it. It was what they had, and as such, it must suffice.

His worries drifted to their audience with Herod. Like all kings, Herod was capricious, not to be trusted. What should he have said or not said? What danger might they have instigated? Questions plagued him, but dusk was just around the corner, he reminded himself, and the stars always had much to tell.

Just then Melchior stuck his head in the room. "Balt, come out here. You have to see this."

Balthazar groaned and forced himself upright, still smarting from the rough treatment. He splashed water on his face from the bowl in the corner, and then wearily tottered to the door. He was just in time to see a legion of Herod's soldiers marching off into the west, kicking up a cloud of dust in their wake. Caspar and Melchior came out of hiding when the troops were at a safe distance. "That brigand that assaulted us is leading them," Caspar snarled. "He didn't see us."

"What do you suppose that's all about?" A young man sitting on the porch of the inn wondered aloud.

Melchior ignored the young man, but answered the question, addressing his friends in their own language. "My guess is that Herod is trying to find the child before we do." The dust from the soldiers' sandals had settled like an ominous cloud over their hearts. Without another word, Caspar and Melchior retired again to the tavern to finish their supper. Balthazar was too weary to even make the short journey back to the room, so he enjoyed the falling dark on the porch, in the company of the young stranger.

They chatted politely for a while, until the young man excused himself. "My wife just had a baby a few days ago," he explained. "I should bring her some dinner."

Something in Balthazar nudged him. "Wait," he said to the young man. "Where was your child born?"

"Bethlehem," said the young man. "We've just come from there. Have you been?"

"No," Balthazar shook his head, and although he did not know how, he knew in that moment that he would not be going to Bethlehem after all. He noted the room into which the young man disappeared, and he forced his creaky bones into motion and summoned his companions. They stood outside the tavern door in the dark, whispering excitedly as Balthazar related the conversation he had just had. Just then Caspar looked up, and his jaw dropped. Melchior halted mid-sentence as he and Balthazar followed his gaze to the heavens. The new star was no longer hanging in the west, leading them on. It was straight overhead, blazing like a pillar of fire. They stared at one another in the eerie light it produced, and then, as if on a predetermined cue, they scrambled to their room to collect their effects.

*** *** ***

A few minutes later, the Zoroastrians were poised outside the young man's door. Taking a deep breath, Balthazar knocked politely and waited. The man he had chatted with just a few minutes ago opened the door, surprised to see the three of them crowded around the opening. "Oh, hi again," he said uncertainly. "What… can I do for you?" It made him nervous that none of them were looking at him, but *past* him, to where Mary and the baby were nearly asleep.

Balthazar remembered his manners and turned his attention to the young man. "My apologies for the interruption. We seek an audience with you…and your family."

"Look, they're trying to sleep. They're exhausted. Believe me, you don't want the little one to start in again. This is the only time in my life I have cursed the Holy One for not making me deaf. Can you come back tomorrow?"

"My friend," Balthazar put his hand on Joseph's arm, "we have traveled for weeks from Persia just to meet you and your child. Our priestly arts have divined that a baby of great importance has just been born. And we think that baby is yours."

Joseph's eyes widened. "Yes," he said, "I know just what you mean. Well, come in and meet the family. I'm not sure what heroic feats are in store for my son, but you will soon witness for yourself his superhuman lungs. He's a howler, make no mistake."

Mary stirred as the Persians entered. They tried to do it quietly, but their clothes were adorned with metals that clanked and tinkled when they walked. It was a pleasant sound to wake to, and although she was initially startled, Joseph calmed her with a "Shhh, dear, it's all right. The man in the dream has come to these men, too, in his own way. They know. They're here to meet Jesus."

The foreigners knelt before Mary as she rocked the baby on her lap. Their breath caught in their throats and they gazed at the child with evident rapture. The baby, amazingly, gurgled but did not wake. Joseph was grateful for that—he was far easier to adore asleep.

"Gentlemen, let us consult the Urim and Thummim," Balthazar suggested. Caspar shook his head to clear it, and fished around in his shoulder bag. He brought out an embroidered pouch containing two well-worn stones, similar to the ones the Israelites had brought back with them when they left their captivity in Babylon. Today they were embedded in Zachariah's breastplate at the Temple, removed only when matters of grave import had to be discerned. In the Zoroastrian tradition, they were the most traditional and reliable means of divining Ahura Mazda's will.

Mary and Joseph looked on with wonder as Caspar prayed over the stones. For their benefit, he repeated his chief inquiry in Aramaic: "Is this, in fact, the child we seek?" He shook the pouch, and then turned it upside down. The stones fell out, and both of them landed with their crude etchings face up.

"He is." They looked at one another in a surreal state of disbelief. "I don't understand," Melchior breathed wonderingly. He spoke again in Persian, "How could this child be a prince? His parents are peasants!"

"Many a tale we have heard of princes sent off to die because of some curse or other," Caspar suggested, "only to be raised by peasants until heaven deemed them ready to reclaim their thrones." The other two nodded. But then, Caspar had an idea. Praying over the stones, he asked, "Is this child Mithra?" The other two gasped at the blasphemy. But before they could protest the stones had tumbled out, and come to rest one up, one down—a qualified yes.

"He is not Mithra reborn," Balthazar interpreted, "but he is like him, a savior. Mithra, in the old tongue, means *covenant*," he reminded them. "Perhaps this child is another covenant, a new covenant between Mazda and this people, and maybe of others as well." The others nodded breathlessly, knowing in their hearts that his reading was a true one.

Satisfied, they put the stones away and withdrew their humble gifts from their bags. They knelt once again before the child, but addressed Joseph. "We greet you on behalf of the court of his majesty Phraataces, emperor of Persia. In his name we offer these gifts, meager as they are. Gold, as befits a king, for he will rule with the hand of justice," Balthazar breathed, almost in a trance. He unrolled the scarf, revealing more gold than Joseph had ever seen in his life. Mary's eyes grew wide and she looked at Joseph with something like alarm. "Is that for us?" she mouthed. He shrugged and returned his gaze to the priests, who were offering other gifts.

"Myrrh, as befits a physician, for he will heal both the body and the soul. And Frankincense, as befits a priest, for he will mediate for his people before Mazda." Mary and Joseph were speechless. Nobody they knew had this much money or would ever earn this much money, with the possible exception of Zachariah. "I-I-I, I don't know what to say," Joseph stammered.

"Shh…" Balthazar smiled, "there is no need." And then, in hushed reverence, the priests set up a brazier and performed a fire ceremony in the child's honor. When they had finished singing their prayers in their beautiful, harmonious, but strange language, they quickly packed their things away, bowed low, and were gone.

"Joseph," Mary's voice broke the long silence that followed their exit. "What just happened?"

"I'm not sure," he answered, "but I have a feeling that the weirdness is just beginning."

The Lamb of God

Mary stared out the window into the dusty Jerusalem street. A gaggle of Pharisees in their long black robes were arguing, and it was becoming heated. She was too far away to hear what they were saying, and the lazy midmorning light caught the dust they scuffed up in a way that made their animated exchanges look magical, a mystical slow-motion choreography of arm-waving and spittle. Elizabeth, her aunt, leaned over her shoulder to see what had caught her attention. "A little wine, my dear?"

Mary started to turn before her eyes could break away. "What?"

Elizabeth poured for the both of them. "I never trust men who presume to speak for God," she said, handing Mary an ornate cup.

One of the things Mary enjoyed most about their annual visit to the holy city was staying with Elizabeth. For one week out of the year, she could pretend she wasn't poor. In Elizabeth's company she felt like a queen, and it was a feeling she could all too easily get used to.

"My Zachariah never did that." Elizabeth sounded sad for a moment. Her husband had died almost twenty years ago now, but he was very much alive in the conversations in this house. "In fact, when Zachariah heard from God, he never spoke at all." She smiled at her young niece, and consciously lightened the mood. "Tell me how your boys are doing."

"Well, all right. I suppose I should start with James, since there's not much to tell. You remember he was ordained last year? I never see him since he got that post in the little synagogue in Ber-Sheba. He and Rebecca have two daughters, now—"

"Two! That is new!"

"—and still trying for a son, bless him."

"And Judas?"

"I swear, if the Indians are right and we do come back for another round on earth after we die, then Judas is his father reborn. He is a master carpenter. Not married yet, but he can put together a table in his sleep."

"He didn't come with you this year?"

"No, he has a commission that won't wait, and after all, someone has to earn some…money…" she trailed off, not wanting to discuss her poverty. Or her other son, who did not work unless the world was about to end.

"Jesus looks well," Elizabeth brought him up anyway, and topped off their cups.

"Yes, he's well." Mary stared into hers, and watched the oily swirl of color on the wine's surface as it heaved and settled. Like her stomach when she talked about her eldest.

"Oooh, feeling a little touchy about Jesus these days?" Elizabeth asked softly.

"Oh, Liz. I had such dreams for him. There was so much promise. And he's so…" The right word eluded her. Lazy? Insecure? Unsure? Emotional? "He's so…*not* what I thought he would be."

"Well, I know what you mean." If anyone knew how she felt, it was Elizabeth, whose own son had been a terrible disappointment to her. "Both our boys may have abandoned their callings, but at least you have a son at home with you. Heavens, you have two! I've been so bereft since Zachariah died. Sure, I've got money, but what good is it if there's no one to enjoy it with? And Jesus is so good to you. He waits on you hand and foot. Anyone can see that he loves you like there's no tomorrow."

She smiled at Mary and then sat back, sighing heavily. "The Torah reading from John's Bar Mitsvah was still echoing in the air when he took up with those traitors, the Essenes. I'm just glad Zachariah wasn't alive to see it, it would have broken his heart. They are against everything he loved, everything he stood for. John is as good as dead to me. And now look at him—" she waved her arm toward the window, as if they could see clear out to the Jordan river from here. "He's a raving lunatic. Half naked, eating nothing but locusts. Oh, don't get me wrong, dear, your locust cakes are divine, but a man cannot live on locusts alone. What did I ever do to God to deserve such a son?"

"Some say he's Elijah," said Jesus, walking in with an armful of wood for the fire.

"He's not Elijah," Elizabeth spat. "He's nutty as almond butter. And why are you working, dear? That's what servants are for."

"I'm the servant around our house," Jesus said matter-of-factly. Mary looked like she wanted to disappear into her tunic.

"Well, there's no shame in being poor." Elizabeth, noticing, patted her arm. "Only in acting like it."

"Mother," Jesus said, straightening up, "I'm going off for the day."

"Where to?"

"I'm going to see John."

"Like hell you are!" She nearly choked on her wine.

"Mother, he's my cousin. He's famous. I want to see what all the buzz is about."

"Absolutely not." Mary was firm.

"Sorry, Mother, but I'm a thirty-year-old man. I respect your opinion, but I make my own decisions."

"Let him go, Mary," Elizabeth moaned. "Let him gaze upon my shame. Let him see just how crazy the man has become. There's no better preventative to madness, that's what I think. Let him behold the wreckage of a man who betrays his family and his God."

*** *** ***

The sun was high in the heavens when Jesus came in sight of the Jordan. The water looked deceptively languid, but he could see people struggle to keep their feet as they waded out to meet the Baptist.

Jesus would not have recognized him. The boy he remembered egging him on to mischief was nowhere to be seen. In his place was a wild man, sporting a long and tangled beard, with hair just as long and matted hanging off the back of his head. His modesty was barely secured by a mere scrap of a loincloth that at first glance looked for all the world like a patch of impossibly overgrown pubic hair that matched his beard and hairdo in its virulent untidiness.

He was a big man, like his father, but his arms were skinny, testifying to all who cared to notice that his labor was intellectual and prophetic rather than menial. Jesus could see those skinny arms gesticulating in wide, animated arcs long before he could hear the Baptist's words. Just as he reached the pebbly plain that led up to the water, he was finally within earshot of the prophet.

"—be ready," he was saying. "How can you be ready? You've got to be right! The world is a maze of crooked paths. God waits and waits and waits. And you never know when the Kingdom will be upon you."

Jesus took a seat on the pebbles near a pocket of curious onlookers. There were nearly a hundred people, all sitting in little cliques on the riverbank. All of them were straining to hear the prophet, or more likely, straining to understand what the heck he was talking about.

Jesus' brow furrowed with the rest of them. Maybe his great aunt was right. Maybe John *was* mad. He hadn't made a lick of sense yet.

"Any day, now," John bellowed, waving those scarily long and skinny arms of his, "the Son of Man will walk among us. But God is waiting to send his salvation. What is he waiting for, you ask?

He's waiting for you! He's waiting for you to take the meandering paths of your lives and make them a straight highway worthy for a King to trod! Until you do you will never be free of the yoke of the oppressor. For I tell you true, it is not Rome that holds you in bondage, it is your own sins!"

The crowd murmured and squirmed. Obviously they were curious, but John had not yet won them over. Then Jesus noticed a smaller gathering on the opposite shore. These nodded with every word the prophet spoke. *These must be his disciples,* Jesus thought, *the true believers.*

"You are the oppressor, and you are the oppressed!" John shouted. "And only you can liberate yourselves! And until you do, our people will never know peace. The Kingdom of Heaven is even now poised above us, pregnant with salvation. The world groans with the pains of her labor. You are the midwife, but until you tend to your duties, the child of promise cannot be born! Midwives, come and wash yourselves, and prepare to deliver! Take all of your greed, your deceit, your willful defiance of God and his law, and let the river carry it away into the outer darkness. Just as Aaron placed the sins of the people upon the head of the scapegoat that carried them into the wilderness, come to this river, empty yourselves of your rebellion, and let it carry away your pride, your hatred, your apathy, your collusion, your—"

He stopped suddenly, staring right at Jesus. He squinted, rubbed his eyes, and looked again. "Cousin, is that you?"

Jesus waved. "Hi, John."

"You look great."

"Well, um…you look kind of scary."

John laughed from deep in his belly. He turned to address his disciples. "Hey, everyone, this is my cousin. The gentlest boy I ever knew. Used to nurse hurt birds and lizards back to health all the time. We used to call him God's little lamb. Are you still the gentle one?"

Everyone turned to Jesus. Jesus was aware that everyone was

looking at him. He had never felt more on the spot. "Uh, yeah... If anyone is looking for someone to beat up, I'm your guy."

"Have you come to be baptized, Cousin?"

"I came to see you. And I came to hear you preach. But I'm fresh out of sins. I wouldn't want to wash away any of the good stuff, you know." This got a laugh from the crowd, who had apparently decided Jesus was all right, and turned their attention back to John, whom they were reasonably sure was still a lunatic.

"How about the rest of you? The Kingdom of God cannot arrive in power until you are ready to receive it! Make straight what is crooked! Set free the captive within you! Create a Kingdom worthy of its King, but begin with your own heart! Who will be baptized? Who wants to be made clean? Who would hasten the arrival of the Kingdom!"

To Jesus' amazement, several people got up and picked their way over the stones toward the Baptist. One by one, John asked them to speak their sins over the water, then he grabbed them and violently shoved them under the current. "Clean! Be made clean!" He shouted, and then he released them, and sputtering, they fought for their footing and shambled toward shore, shivering and shaken.

As Jesus watched them, he struggled with a strange stirring in his breast. He felt oddly drawn to the Baptist. He wasn't at all sure he believed what the Baptist was saying, but in his soul he detected a persistent nudging that compelled him to be part of what his cousin was doing.

When the last of the volunteers had made their way back to the bank, John once again addressed the crowd. "Anyone else?" he cried.

"What the heck," Jesus said under his breath, and rose to meet his cousin. John's face registered surprise. "Are you sure about this, Jesus?"

"Nope. Do me before I think better of it."

"But you said you have no sin to wash away. If that is true, then I am not worthy to baptize you—maybe you should baptize me!" John joked, mussing his hair in the same rough and playful way Jesus remembered so fondly. He might look like a barbarian, but he was the same old John underneath all that grime and hair.

"Speak your sins, cousin."

Jesus hesitated and swallowed hard. No one but John was close enough to hear. "Jesus. Your sins."

"I am so sorry I have been such a disappointment to my mother. She had such hopes for me. And I broke her heart." Jesus might as well have plunged a dagger into John. The Baptist staggered and nodded unconsciously, waiting for Jesus to continue. "It kills me every time I look at her and see her sadness. I know I have failed, but I don't know what I should have done differently. God forgive me."

The Baptist's face had drained of color, and his own conscience struck at him violently. Distractedly he shook his head, now impossibly ashen, and grabbing Jesus by the front of his tunic, plunged him in over his head. The icy deep swirled around Jesus' ears, so cold it made his head hurt. His lungs had just begun to ache for air when the stone grip of the Baptist released him, and he bobbed up, his feet searching for firm purchase.

He had just stood up again when thunder cracked so loud he and the Baptist both nearly jumped out of their skins. Instinctively they both looked up, and wondering at the cloudless sky, they saw a dove circling about twenty feet above them. Then, without warning, the bird turned and dove straight down towards them. Their jaws both gaped in wonder, and they were entirely unprepared when the dove flew into Jesus' mouth and lit in his throat. A blue light exploded from out of his mouth, blinding them both for a long impossible moment.

"Holy crap!" John exclaimed. "What the hell was that?"

Thunder again pealed out, and Jesus and John grasped at each other's arms to keep their balance in the rushing water. A voice tumbled out from the thunder, proclaiming, "This is my son, whom I love dearly. Today I have given birth to you. Listen to him!" The thunder faded and John and Jesus hovered precariously, gripping each other's forearms for dear life. Jesus felt faint but a strange sweetness on his tongue kept him present.

Their mouths were still unconsciously open, but now they were dripping. John sucked his mouth closed and then spat in his palm. "Milk." He said incredulously, looking at his hand.

"Honey," said Jesus, trailing sticky golden cobwebs between his fingers and lips.

"...God...damn," breathed John.

Jesus didn't even rebuke his blasphemy. The people on the shore looked at them with a mixture of amusement and concern, apparently oblivious to the theophany that had nearly overcome them.

"You two all right?" one of John's followers asked. "You should maybe sit in the shade for a while, don'tcha think?"

Jesus and John shuffled together toward the far shore where his disciples had risen to their feet and were now buzzing with mild concern. As soon as the water was shallow enough they both sat down and vacantly stared at each other. Unconsciously, Jesus sucked at the honey on his fingers as he swayed back and forth like a reed in the wind.

∗∗∗   ∗∗∗   ∗∗∗

Supper had ended, but Jesus had barely touched the wooden plate John's disciples had prepared for him. He huddled in a blanket and rocked back and forth. John had recovered somewhat, and after bidding his cousin good night, had retired to his cave. John's followers swarmed here and there, whispering worriedly about their teacher's odd behavior and the stranger he called God's lamb.

Few noticed when a young man joined Jesus by the fire. For a while they stared silently together. Then, tentatively, the young man spoke. "I saw it."

Jesus looked up, snapping out of his private thoughts, and noticed the young man for the first time. "What?" he said.

"I saw it," The young man said again. "I saw the bird fly into your mouth. I heard that voice. I saw the light." Jesus turned and looked at him. "I'm not the only one who saw it, either," the young man added.

As if on cue, another figure emerged from the shadows and sat close to the young man. He was a little older, and had a well-kept beard and an impressive scar on his cheek. "I saw it, too," he said. This new stranger turned to face Jesus. "Are you a prophet?" he asked.

"No. John's the prophet."

"Then who are you?"

"I'm a carpenter. A bad one. What I really am is a failure."

The young man's brow bunched and he tried to size Jesus up. Finally he announced, "I don't care if you're the Queen of Babylon, I'm going to follow you."

"Don't waste your time," Jesus said, looking at the fire. "I'm not worth following."

"Hey, if I get to see more trippy stuff like that, you are."

"I didn't do that."

"Who did? John? I've been following him off and on for five years. The only miraculous thing about him is his verbosity and his obnoxious gaseous emissions."

"It's his diet," the man with the scar explained. "Bugs and sweets. Powerful bad combination. I tell you this from experience." He clutched at his gut and feigned a painful spasm.

"Where do you live?"

"Why do you want to know?" Jesus returned.

"I told you. We're coming with you."

"I don't think so. My mother won't have it. The last time I brought a friend home—"

"We'll sleep in the yard," the scarred man interrupted him. "We don't care what you say. We've heard John so often we can mouth the words along with him. 'The Kingdom of heaven is coming, the Kingdom of heaven is coming.'" The other chimed in the second time around, and they both laughed.

"Oh, I'm so sick of that," the young one said.

"We know what John's all about," the scarred one continued, "but we never heard the voice of God until today. So you can play at your humility bit all you want. We're still coming with you."

Jesus sighed, and felt an unstoppable sadness begin to emerge from deep in his belly. Then he felt another stirring; his throat swelled like he was going to cry, and a voice that was not his own was pushing at his lips. He felt momentarily dissociated, like he was witnessing the scene from above, from outside his own body. With wonder he watched his own mouth open, and the words of another tumbled out.

"John's wrong," the voice said. The men by the fire looked up at him, with surprise, for his voice had taken on an authority they had not heard from this slight and insecure stranger before. "The Kingdom of Heaven isn't coming. It's here."

The **Wedding** at **Cana**

The morning sun shot through the little courtyard with the force of a revelation. It was the second hour, and the air was still cool, the leaves a little wet. It was Deborah's wedding day, and Mary was in the house washing up. Jesus wandered the courtyard, giving her some privacy, enjoying the brisk feeling that morning always gave him. It was his favorite time of the day.

He was circumambulating the little yard, with his hands clasped behind him, sniffing, feeling the sun on his beard, enjoying. Or *trying* to enjoy. He hadn't slept well and had awakened with a sick feeling of dread that he could not pin on anything. So he carried it like an awkwardly-shaped package—easily, but with some discomfort.

Just then he caught sight of a beetle marching from one end of the courtyard to the other. It was black and shiny, about the size of his thumbnail, and appeared to be driven by some transcendent sense of purpose. It was relentless in its trek, and Jesus squatted to get a better look at him.

"Where are you going in such a hurry, little beastie?" he asked it. "Are you afraid you'll be late? What could be so pressing for a creature who still lives in the Garden?"

The beetle did not stop to answer. It was traveling faster than Jesus expected, and he found himself doing a duck-walk to keep up with it and still be close enough to converse.

Just as the little creature approached the halfway point, Mary came out of the house carrying her washbasin.

"Mother, let me get that." Jesus rose when he saw her.

"I've got it, you keep—" she realized then that he had been squatting when she first came out "—you keep doing whatever it was you were doing."

She poured the water out, and Jesus wondered at her strength, her self-reliance. Ever since Father had died, she had seemed to inherit his strength of body as well as character.

The beetle caught his eye again, and he watched with a little thrill of horror as he realized that the water from Mary's tub was racing straight for him. Or rather, he was marching straight for it. "He is still safe," Jesus thought. "He could stop or go a different direction." But the little beast seemed determined and sped straight into the path of the water. The water collided with him, and Jesus saw the little black legs flailing furiously. The little river carried him away, and bore him out of the yard, into the alley.

His mother did not notice this little drama and looked at him, still squatting in the yard, wondering if her worst fears were right, if perhaps he were mad. "Are you going to wash before we head over?" asked his mother.

"Is that a hint?" asked Jesus.

"If you wash, I'll make breakfast for you."

"You'll make breakfast anyway."

"Not this morning I won't."

"You're a hard taskmaster, Mother."

"Here's the tub."

It was hard to predict what his mother would do. At first he thought she was annoyed with him this morning, but when he had finished washing—and carefully disposed of his water so as not to carry off any wildlife—he found that she had prepared a breakfast fit for a feast-day.

There was porridge, of course, which was all he was really expecting this morning. But she had also soaked some smoked fish so it was soft and salty, and there was a bowl full of figs and dates. He sucked the pits from a couple of dates and dropped them into the porridge. His mother had a fondness for biscuits made from dried locust flour and had just made a batch up. He had always thought they were a little gritty, but he was used to them, and they had honey in the house, which covered a multitude of culinary sins. He poured a little on the biscuits and a lot in the porridge.

His mother set a little cup of wine by his elbow and sat across from him. She grabbed a couple of biscuits and picked at them while he ate. "When are you going to start?"

"Hmm?" he looked up. *Oh, dear,* he thought. *Here we go again.*

"When are you going to do—whatever you are here to do?"

He chewed and considered her in the soft morning light coming through the window. She was still beautiful, he did not even see her age. They had had this conversation before—many times. The best policy, he had found, was to simply listen and nod and seem sympathetic. And to try not to take it personally. He knew she considered him a bit of a failure. He was certainly a misfit. He considered himself a happy misfit, though, and he smiled at this thought. Except that it wasn't true—his future hung over his head like a thundercloud, and he was always waiting for the lightning to strike.

"What are you smiling about?" She rocked back in her seat. "Are you making fun of me?"

"Oh, mother, no, of course not. A man is entitled to his own thoughts."

"You never listen to me. Your time is running out. You're thirty—most men don't live to see forty. I can't stand to see you—to see it all—" She wanted to say, "All I've been through," but she didn't want to say something so selfish.

So they sat there while he chewed and the knot in her stomach twisted tighter. "Are those friends of yours coming? Those

John people? It seems to me that you're spending an awful lot of time with them."

He gave her a smile and reached for another biscuit. "They're good men," he said.

"They're deadbeats and radicals. I'm afraid you'll go off to the desert again. That you'll become like John. When he quit his job at the temple and went out to that desert, it broke Elizabeth's heart. I'm just glad Zachariah was dead already."

Then she realized what she had just said, and looked cowed for a minute. "I didn't mean that. You know what I mean."

"I know what you mean. It's all right, mother. I've done the desert thing. And I came back, didn't I?"

"You're not back," she said bitterly. "You left a part of yourself out there. I can see it in your eyes. You're restless."

He stopped chewing and felt the knot in his stomach start to hurt. He really hated this, and wondered if it was the lot common to all sons.

"Jesus, God wants you to do something great. Truly great!" she said, looking like she was about to cry. "But I'm afraid that at any minute you're just going to cut and run. That you are going to say 'no' to God."

He wanted to say, "How can anyone say 'no' to God?" but he knew his tone would be too testy, so he shut up and tore at his fish.

He was silent for several minutes, and that was when she knew she had pushed too far. She had made him mad. When he was really angry, he just clammed up. She went to the sideboard to clean up. At least this was better than what Susannah had to deal with from her son—he hit her when she angered him. She could endure silence. It was his absence that scared her. She had hoped he would marry, have children, become a great teacher, attract students to his yeshiva.

Instead, he was a middle-aged man with no prospects. He hung around with other men, seemingly unemployed, the kind that followed John. His other brothers were out of the house, with jobs and wives. James was rich, Judas was struggling, but independent, as he always had been. Even Salome, her youngest, was betrothed and living happily with Elizabeth until her big wedding day. But Jesus was a different animal, and seemed to be cut from different cloth than his siblings. She needed to believe that Jesus could still be great. She had suffered so much, after all. And the angel—the angel had said so. Life seemed suddenly so unfair.

He had time, she told herself. And she would have hope. Joseph was depending on her. It was up to her to support him until…until…until he did…whatever it was he was supposed to do. She watched her son play with a bone at the table and swallowed back the bile in her throat.

When they arrived at the wedding, most of the guests were already in evidence. Jesus had found his friends—who *hadn't* washed this morning, Mary noted with a snort. A little gaggle of them gathered in one corner, arguing Torah, laughing and teasing that little one whose name she couldn't remember because it was a gentile name. *How could a parent do that?* she asked herself.

"Mary, you look beautiful, my dear." She groaned inwardly but turned and gave the speaker a gracious smile. Deborah's father bowed a shallow bow, and beamed at her. "It's a beautiful day, and my Deborah is a beautiful bride."

"Yes, Simon, she is beautiful." She stopped and looked across the yard at the bride. She was drunk with self-importance, and the sun seemed to be shining on her alone. *It is exactly as it should be on her wedding day*, Mary thought, and allowed herself a tingle of excitement looking forward to Salome's wedding in the fall.

"Is your son giving you trouble? You look annoyed." Was she really so transparent? She gave him a smile, and shook her head. "He's fine. Just distant." Simon was sweet, but was also subtly courting her. He was a sweaty, oafish man who did not treat women with the deference Mary had become accustomed to from her own late husband, and so she kindly rebuffed his advances whenever they were made, which was often several times a year.

"He's an odd one, that's for sure." Those people who liked to murmur about Jesus' odd-timed birth and seeming illegitimacy were mostly dead and buried now. Few people whispered "bastard" behind his back anymore, but everyone thought it. And of course, everyone thought Mary a little loose because of this history, true or not. It had probably fueled Simon's fantasies for years.

"Don't let me keep you, Simon," Mary said to him kindly. "There are more guests to greet."

"You could greet them with me," he gave her a kind and vulnerable look, and then turned away, embarrassed.

She wasn't sure if this was an oblique proposal or if he simply wanted a woman to lean on today, since he was losing his daughter. His nervousness betrayed that it was probably the former, but she acted as if it were the latter. She took his arm and steered him towards the crowd whooping and laughing in the center of the yard. "Let's mingle," she whispered, and pretended not to notice when he wiped at his eyes.

The ceremony itself was splendid. There wasn't a cloud in the sky. The sun shone through the huppah and transfigured the couple as the priest pronounced his blessing. Micah, Deborah's betrothed, smashed the cup, a great cheer went up from the assembled throng, and suddenly she was his wife.

The menfolk grabbed Micah, tore him from his new bride's grasp, and lifted him on their shoulders to parade him around the courtyard. The women surrounded Deborah and showered her with flowers and kisses and flattery.

Jesus and his friends sprinted around the circle, passing Micah from shoulder to shoulder, singing and clapping and calling for wine. The dancing went on for hours.

Mary watched her son as a darksome longing moved in her breast. Except for the beard, she could have been watching him at Esther's wedding twenty years ago. He danced with the same abandon, laughted with the same ferocity. He seemed just as disinterested in women and just as devoted to his playmates as ever he was then. "He's a well-educated little boy," she thought, and then banished it for fear tears would come in its wake.

"What??" she heard Simon bellow. "How can that be? Are you trying to ruin me?" She shot one more glance at her fool boy dancing like David before the ark, and turned to see what the matter was. At least, unlike David, Jesus was keeping his clothes on.

Simon was shaking with rage and sweating like a new bladder hung out to dry. "How can there be no more wine?" The servant looked like he might crumble beneath Simon's verbal assault.

"Master, I'm sorry. We ordered plenty. There were simply more guests than we expected."

Mary felt a twinge of guilt as she thought of Jesus' friends, who had not been invited, but who had come along anyway, simply because he had. She was about to say something when she realized that Jesus had only brought three of them along, and they were not alone responsible for the shortage. Then she thought of how much Jesus could pack away when he let himself go, and pursed her lips, uncertain what to do.

"Simon, has the wine run out, then?"

"I'm sure I ordered enough. What could have happened? Deborah will never forgive me." He paced back and forth like a caged animal, wringing his hands with worry. He had to make a plan. He could send some servants to market, but it would take them some time, and then everyone would know. Then suddenly the crowd was calling for him. It was traditional for the father of the bride to lead off one of the dances, and he looked like an antelope torn between two lions, panic flickering in his eyes.

"Simon, dance," Mary told him. "I'll take care of this."

Jesus was coming around the bend, hair flying wet and streaming with sweat. She waved at him and caught his attention. "Come here," she mouthed, and he nodded, continuing his dance until he reached her.

"Having a good time, Mother?"

"We have a problem," she said simply.

"Nobody likes to hear that," he laughed.

She chewed on her lip and struggled with how to approach him. She could send him off to the market with instructions to be speedy and circumspect so that the other guests would not catch on. You could not trust a servant to be careful—they were always looking for ways to make their masters look foolish. Jesus could do it, and properly, and quickly. But another option nagged at her. She remembered how, as a child, he would adjust the wood in Joseph's shop. Joseph would scold him, tell him he needed to learn to do things properly, but then he would muss his hair and kiss him on the cheek when Mary wasn't looking.

Judas was the born carpenter in the family. James cared only for books and Jesus, well, Jesus was quite simply terrible at it. But he *could* make those boards grow. And the bird—she thought often about the little bird Jesus had made out of clay, how he had breathed on it and threw it into the air; how she had almost fallen over in a dead faint when with an audible "crack" the wings unfolded and caught the current of the air and flew up and out of sight.

Jesus saw the look in her eyes and steeled himself. "It's time, baby," she said with finality. Jesus didn't know what she was talking about, but the look in her eyes told him that the corner he had not dared to turn was looming before him.

James is the rabbi, not me, he thought. *I'm...I'm nothing. I do child's tricks, I dream, I talk to God, but I am no rabbi. Men will not follow me. Don't make me do this.* But when he opened his mouth, all he said was, "What do you want me to do?"

She looked at him, her frail little bird. He was not going to leave the nest on his own. *It is my duty to push him*, she told herself. *God demands it.* It was a hollow rationalization, and she swooned a little at the thought of it.

"Simon has run out of wine, and Deborah will never forgive him if she finds out."

"So send some servants to market."

She gave him that look. "They'll take all day and you know it."

"What do you want me to do?" he asked again.

"You can make wine." He stared at her as if she had suddenly revealed she was Moses himself.

Yes, he could probably do that. But then people would talk, people would know. They would come looking for him, asking for miracles of their own. They would make assumptions. His quiet life, it would all be over. Right now he was a ne'er-do-well. If he did this, he would be like John. He would be called Rabbi and master and people would want things from him.

He considered his mother carefully. Was this his own mother pushing him towards his doom? Or was this Satan in disguise? He looked around the courtyard. Mary thought he looked like a cornered cat, seeking an escape route. Actually he was looking for another Mary, his real mother, some evidence that this was the Deceiver standing in front of him and not his own dear mother asking him to end his wonderful life.

"Love," she said, and brushed his cheek. "It's time."

No, that was his mother all right. He caught her hand and held it. Maybe it wasn't Satan speaking through her. Maybe it *was* God. Maybe it was.

Just then a dove cooed and lit on the ground. It walked in a circle and pecked at the dust. And then it looked up, straight into Jesus' eyes. He felt like it had been pecking at his soul.

He turned to a servant who was passing by. "Can you fill those jars with water?"

He pointed at the empty wine pots in the corner of the patio. "Yes, but why? There's plenty of water."

"Just do as he says," Mary commanded in her voice that permitted no argument.

The servant shrugged, picked up one of the jars, and started towards the well. Mary caught the attention of some other servants and enlisted them in the task. Quickly, several jars had been filled and returned to the patio.

"Jesus, what are you doing? You're missing out on the big dance!" His friend blew in from the throng breathlessly.

"Go ahead, I'll be there in a moment," he smiled wickedly. "Just getting some more wine."

His friend smiled approvingly and leaped away again, taking Jesus' grin with him. For a moment he just stood there staring into space, wondering what to do next. There were the jars, full of water, waiting for him to...to do what? He looked at Mary uncertainly. "I don't know what to do."

"What did you do when you made the bird real? What did you do when you lengthened those boards? Or when you found my necklace last year?"

"I prayed."

"So pray."

Jesus held his hand out over the jars, lifted his eyes to heaven and began a blessing in Hebrew. And then there was no going back. It had begun. He wasn't her little boy anymore. He had set forth on whatever painful track Simeon had warned her of so many years ago at his bris.

Before he had finished blessing the jars, she felt sick, guilty, scared. She reached for the wall to support herself as her head swam. Jesus asked for cups and dipped one into one of the jars. He gave it to one of the servants and said, "Here, take this to Simon. Tell him we found more wine under the stairs." He winked at the servant, who stared in awe at the red liquid in the cup.

"Today, if it's not too much trouble," Jesus added. The servant nodded and rushed off.

Then her son who was not her son handed her a cup and forced a smile that she imagined said, "You asked for it."

She was afraid to look in the cup he gave her. In that moment she would have done anything, given anything, for it to have been only water. She forced a smile—a bitter grimace, and she raised the cup to her lips.

It tasted like blood.

A **Resurrection**

The sun had stung at his eyes all day, and now that night had come they hurt. He rubbed at them and squinted at the campfire Andrew had just built. The fire was small, but that was fine. It was more for conviviality than for warmth, and they weren't cooking anything. Dinner was simple, as it usually was when they were traveling—dried, salted chickpeas, figs, and bread, bought from the last village they had passed. Mary handed him the rough bag with their food in it. He smiled at her.

As his companions finished their preparations for the night, they wandered over to the fire and, with satisfied grunts, took their places around it. He was tired, and he didn't feel like teaching. He felt like hearing a story. "Who's got a story?" he asked.

No one said anything. "I've got a question I've been thinking about all day," John said. Jesus sighed, and his heart fell. *No story tonight*, he thought. John didn't wait for his acknowledgment, but just plunged in. "Will the dead really be resurrected? Or is that just a symbol? The Pharisees say it's real, as we all know, since they won't shut up about it. But at the temple they say no, it's just a symbol. Well, which is it?"

"The temple priests are the real authorities," Thaddeus said. "God has given them their authority, and we ought to listen to them. Who are the Pharisees, after all? They appoint themselves."

"Whoa!" a collective groan of surprise rose up from the group of friends. Even Jesus couldn't help smiling.

"*Those* are words to pick a fight," John said. "*Our* rabbi's rabbi was a Pharisee, remember."

Thaddeus looked over at Jesus, a bit sheepishly. Jesus flashed back on old Reuben—so passionate for the Law, so cantankerous. He realized he still grieved for his friend. His heart hurt, his eyes stung, and his bones were weary from walking. He knew he was not long for an upright position.

"The Greeks say that the body isn't important," Small James noted. "They say the spirit lives on, but the body remains in the dust."

"Since when are the Greeks an authority on anything?" asked John.

"A lot of people put stock in their philosophers," James answered. John spat. "They *do*," James protested.

"Well, which is it?" Peter repeated. He looked at Jesus. They all did. Jesus sighed. He *so* very badly wanted to hear a story. Teaching could wait for another day—especially teaching on a topic like *this* one. He almost said this, but before he could get the words out, Mary spoke up.

"I have another question for the rabbi," she said. "An *important* one."

Peter issued a groan of protest, obviously stung by Mary's implied criticism. This made most everyone else smile. Peter and Mary had become rivals for Jesus' attention, and he tired of their constant push and pull. He sighed again.

"Rabbi," Mary continued, ignoring Peter, "yesterday, you counseled that woman we met by the village gate to marry 'before it was too late.' Do you recall?" He raised his eyebrows, so she continued. "It made me angry. Is it too late for me? I am much older than she is."

Several of the others around the fire shifted nervously. Salome, Jesus' sister, was traveling with them on this trip, and she looked up at her brother expectantly. "I didn't say that," Jesus said, but he knew it wasn't an answer.

This was not lost on Mary, but she didn't dwell on it. Obviously this was not her main point. "She made me remember my mother," Mary continued. "When my father died, she and I were turned out onto the street. My mother became a prostitute in order to feed me. You say that the God of Israel is a God of justice for the orphan and the widow. Where was the justice for my mother?"

Jesus scowled at the fire. A few of the men tittered and mumbled between themselves. Jesus could feel the eyes of Mary and his sister upon him. He did not look up.

"A widowed woman should go to her husband's brother's house," Thaddeus said.

"My father had no brothers," Mary answered.

"Then she should go to her father's house," Thaddeus retorted, beginning to sound defensive.

"My mother's father was dead," Mary said.

"Let her sons take care of her, then," Andrew said.

"And if she has no sons?" No one said anything to that. "You see, this is precisely my question," Mary explained. "The Law of Moses says that our people must provide for widows and orphans, but it seems this Law is only honored when there is a man for a woman to cling to."

"This is blasphemy," Peter decided.

"Why?" Mary protested. "Why is it blasphemy? It happens all the time. It is not wrong to ask a question! If so, every man who's ever entered a yeshiva is a blasphemer! Rabbi, I want to know why the Law of Moses does not provide for women who have no men. Why does God not find us worthy of protection by ourselves? Why may we not stand alone—as circumstances often insist we do—and still be honored by the Law?"

"Well, *you* do all right, and you don't have a man," Thaddeus said. Jesus flashed him an angry look—he was edging toward insult.

"*I* have money," Mary said. But no one spoke of where she

had gotten it. No one dared. There was a long silence in which the fire popped and cracked. "Well, rabbi?" Mary prompted him. "You are the expert on the Law. What do you say?"

Jesus got up and stretched. "The Law says that rest is holy. I'm going to find some." And at that, he ignored their howls of protest and made his way to a soft spot he'd picked out earlier. He didn't look back, either. He didn't want to see the fire in Mary's accusing eyes.

Breakfast was a quiet affair. They packed up soon after sunup and hit the road. Jesus was quiet this morning. He wasn't exactly avoiding Mary and Salome, but he didn't seek them out, either. Mary knew enough to give him some space. It was good, because he needed it. Her questions were good ones. He wondered if it had simply not occurred to Moses what to do in situations like the one Mary's mother found herself in. Yet, surely there were several such cases when Moses led the people.

As he so often did, he probed the edges of the Law in his mind. He turned over what Moses sought to accomplish, then he thought about what God most desired. He pondered the practicality of alternative ideas. Mary seemed to have asked a very simple question, and yet the answer was so complex that he could not find a way through it. Not yet, anyway. He wished he could sit at Moses' feet and ask him, just as Mary had done last night. Would Moses be any better prepared to answer than he had?

Near lunchtime they approached Nain. "Just in time," Jesus said to himself, as his stomach began to rumble. As they drew near to the city gates, they heard the sound of wailers. Jesus frowned. Funerals were common, of course, but they were always sad. About the time they arrived at the gates, the funeral procession passed through them.

Jesus watched the body, wrapped in white linen carried out into the hot desert sun. Behind the body, Jesus saw a woman who must have been either the wife or the mother of the deceased. Jesus saw a local man nearby, probably a merchant by the looks of his clothes, standing respectfully while the procession passed. Jesus drew alongside him and asked, "Someone you knew?"

The man glanced at Jesus, and gave a sad smile. "Not well. People spoke well of him. But he was young. Too young."

Jesus nodded. "So that's his mother, there?"

The man nodded his agreement. "That's her. Terrible situation. Widow. No relatives. Her son was her only means of support. Don't know what's going to happen to her now."

Jesus felt like someone had just punched him in the stomach. The very situation that Mary had been describing was being played out before them once again. The same problem that he had been turning over in his mind for the past four hours, with no answer, and here it was. It was not an artifact of the past, like Mary's mother's story. It was not hypothetical, like so many of the things argued over in the yeshivas. Here was a real woman facing real death, all because there was no man to protect her, to make her "legitimate" in the eyes of the Law. The injustice of it rose up in his throat like bile. He bit back on it and swallowed. His fists clenched. He felt helpless.

Without thinking he ran up and into the road to block the path of the procession. The mourners bumped into each other, and the pallbearers began to shout at him to get out of the way. Jesus held up his hands. "Stay right here," he commanded them.

"And who are you that we should obey you?" asked one of the pallbearers.

Jesus ignored him and approached the man's mother. She looked up at him in confusion and fear. Her cheeks were wet with tears. Jesus' heart broke for her. "Please don't cry," he said. "There's no reason to be afraid."

The woman looked at him as if he were crazy. He saw in her eyes grief for her son, but also terror for her own future. The same terror Mary's mother had faced. Jesus wanted to take her into his arms and hold her close, to comfort her as he did his own sister, but that would not have been seemly. Instead, he smiled at her—a sad, comforting smile. He turned and commanded the pallbearers. "Set him down."

The men looked at each other uncertainly, but they obeyed. Once the body was on the ground, Jesus grabbed the sheet that wound around the body, and he began to unwrap it.

People began to shout at him angrily, but he ignored them. The woman screamed, but he only smiled at her reassuringly. Having uncovered the man's face, Jesus looked at him. The merchant was right, he was young—about ten years younger than Jesus himself.

Jesus leaned down and said to the body, "Young man, I want you to listen to me now. It's time to get up."

The young man's eyes fluttered. They opened. He blinked. He jerked into a sitting position and screamed. "It's okay," Jesus said, reassuringly. "You're safe. You're home. Your mother is here."

The woman let out a wail, and fell upon her son, clinging to him and weeping uncontrollably. Jesus rose, feeling tired again. He looked over at his companions and saw their eyes wide. Several of them were open-mouthed. His own sister looked like she was about to scream. Mary crossed her arms and looked at him darkly.

He breathed deep and stepped over to where they were standing. He touched John on the shoulder. "You have been answered," Jesus said. He saw recognition flash in John's eyes as he remembered his question from the night before regarding resurrection. Jesus turned to Mary and grimaced. "But I'm afraid you are not."

"You fixed it *for her*," Mary said bitterly. "But you didn't *fix it.*"

"I'm sorry," he said.

Her eyes stung at him worse than the sun.

Lord of the Sabbath

It was a particularly sweltering sabbath. Now on weekdays, none of us much minded the heat, especially back when we were workers. My brother James and I, and Andrew and Peter, too, are fishermen, and fond of hot sun and rippling breezes off the Galilean Sea. But we were not working now. We had left the synagogue a little while ago and we were winding our way through the fields, taking a shortcut to the far end of town. Jesus and Peter were walking a little bit ahead of us, discussing a point of Law with all the fervor of young rabbinical students. Thomas and I were behind them. We didn't talk much that day. I think perhaps that was why we were walking together. We enjoyed each other's quiet presence. Either that or Thomas found me less annoying than anyone else that day.

I heard scraps of conversation from the others behind me, almost exclusively on the subject of food. "With what?" I heard Judas snap. I guessed that someone had suggested we buy some bread. "I wouldn't mind a scrap about now, eh, Thomas?" I offered. He coughed, sniffed and looked around. This is as close to an admission of hunger as anyone was likely to get from Thomas. Not that he was always a grumpy sort, just *closed*, if you know what I mean. Only Jesus really seemed to know what he was thinking, and he teased him mercilessly.

"John," Jesus called back. I skipped ahead a couple of steps.

"Yes, Rabbi," I answered.

"What's all the mumbling about back there?" He was smirking a little, and by the look on Peter's face I guessed that the lumbering Galilean was stumped again by the Rabbi's logic.

"Well, it's getting past noon. We're sort of hungry."

He nodded and stopped. "Me, too, I guess." He waited for the others to catch up. "Sorry about that," he said to us. "We just get started, and you know…" Of course we did. How quickly the hours passed as we hung on his every word, revealing new wonders in the everyday world around us. Glimpses of glory in every speck of dust. A glance at Peter confirmed that he was still lost in his own world of thoughts. Jesus bent over and caught a handful of wheat and rubbed his hands together briskly, separating the meat from the sheaf. "Here, Peter," he grabbed the fisherman's hand and dropped the grains of wheat into it. "Eat, it will help you think." Peter stared at his hand but continued to be oblivious to the rest of the world. Jesus pointed to his head and then made bird motions with his hands and we all laughed at his joke at Peter's expense. Peter was certainly with the birds.

Jesus sat down cross-legged and began rubbing more wheat kernals and popping them into his mouth, chewing noisily. We did the same, enjoying the gentle breeze and the nutty taste of crunchy grain. And as we talked about nothing in particular it came home to me how the simplest things were so full of joy. Was it the Rabbi who made it so? I can't imagine sitting in a hot field in the full sun eating raw wheat being much of a meaningful experience. And yet at that moment I didn't want to be anywhere else in the whole wide world.

"We can have a proper dinner later," Jesus said between mouthfuls. "This'll take the edge off some, eh?" He smiled.

"Oh, Peter," Bartholomew piped up, "can you tactfully ask Judith not to use us to try out new recipes? Last night was almost… well, revolting."

"What an ingrate!" Andrew squealed.

Peter seemed to be conscious now and he chuckled. "No one forced you to eat." Judith was his wife, and frequently cooked for us.

"One learns better when one is fed," Bartholomew snapped.

"Oh, I don't know," I said, rubbing wheat in my own hands, "I think that maybe a month of Judith's fish pie is a greater spiritual discipline than fasting."

Jesus choked on his food in spite of his efforts not to laugh. It was a very good day. It was days like this that made us all feel close. Like family, maybe. Like James and I, but different, stronger. Like one body almost.

After a little while, we were on our feet and off again towards the white-washed buildings at the edge of town. As we approached we became aware of several black-clad figures that stood with their arms folded, staring at us. Pharisees. We all became a little tense. Jesus' pace didn't falter, but his eyes narrowed, and I imagine he must have been thinking hard. Dark clouds rolled in upon my perfect day.

"How dare you!" shouted one of them, when we were within hearing range.

"How dare you encourage your men to sin!"

"How dare you accuse me of something I have not done," Jesus answered quietly. There were five of them, all with faces like granite. Jesus would say something similar about their hearts.

"It is forbidden to work on the Sabbath! We have seen you harvest wheat and eat it. We have seen them do the same after you. You are an abomination to Jacob. What do you say for yourself? How can you answer God's Law?"

Jesus reached the side of the narrow street and sat in the shade of a house. "Have you ever read," he asked, looking up at them and shielding his eyes with his hand, "what David did when they were hungry and had nothing? Remember how he and his men entered the tabernacle and ate the consecrated bread that was reserved for the priests alone?"

The Pharisees shifted from one foot to the other and had a look on their faces which plainly said "What new trickery is this?" Peter began a grin on one side of his mouth and looked at

Jesus with something more than love. He began to make a public show of picking his teeth.

"Well," continued Jesus, "he gave this sacred bread to his friends. And did even one of them drop dead from the eating? No. My friends, you have it all backwards. People were not made for the Law. The Law was made for people. You put so much work into keeping the Sabbath that you defeat its purpose: to rest."

He put his head back against the cool wall and sighed patiently. "Therefore, the Son of Man is Lord even of the Sabbath." He opened one eye to see if they were still there. In fact, they were shuffling off mumbling about blasphemy and what could be meant by "Son of Man."

River

you said "I will not eat bread until…"
and then you got that faraway look
every stride brought us closer to the river
simon whispers that you mean to swim it
it is madness, of course, and we all believe it
and you dove into the icy depths
and succumbed…
three heartbeats into eternity
you strained at every muscle
and cradled the far bank
like the bosom of your mother
through our tears we could not see for sure
that it was you
until you called to us: "I'm hungry!"
and I laughed until I had to sit down
because my head was spinning
and then I froze with fear
because I knew that you meant for us
to bring you bread

Palm Sunday

Jerusalem's walls were swelling with pilgrims as people from miles around journeyed to the Holy City to celebrate the Passover the old-fashioned way—at the temple. But it was different this year than last. There was a buzz about the City. Less than a week to go before the big night and already the City was unrecognizable.

The zealots were painting graffiti on the sides of buildings, the Roman soldiers were wary and uneasy, and there was an infectious mania surrounding the Rabbi Jesus Bar Joseph, who was rumored to be on his way. The tension was high, the mood dangerous yet still strangely celebratory.

The disciples, traveling with Jesus, had no inkling of what was happening in the City. They were tired from the constant traveling, and stressed out by Jesus' weird and apocalyptic mood. He kept talking about his death, as if he knew what was going to happen, and had no interest in stopping it. Once Peter had said, "So don't go!" But he got such a tongue-lashing that the others kept their mouths shut and tried not to say anything that might set Jesus off.

Finally they could see the City in the distance. The roads were lined with hundreds of crosses set in the hard-baked earth: a constant reminder to the pilgrims of just who was in charge around here—and a warning: "Don't get any ideas." John was sullen and Peter was spooked, but he didn't say anything. Birds pecked at the corpses that had not yet been taken down and buried. Apparently they had no family and had to rely upon the scavengers for their "burial."

The silence of death hung over the little band as Jerusalem loomed and grew larger, visible now just beyond the suburb of Bethany. Finally Jesus stopped. He turned to the disciples with a quick and elevated look that he used to get when he had just thought of a great joke or had a sudden inspiration. "Andrew, Peter," he said.

"Oh, great," thought Peter, "what now?" What could he possibly be thinking? Did it have anything to do with these crosses? Peter didn't want to stay one more minute than absolutely necessary on this road. It made him feel ritually unclean, but he knew his imagination was getting away with him.

"You guys run on ahead, and just as you reach the village, you'll see a donkey's foal. Get it and bring it back to us. If anyone questions you tell them that the Lord needs it. Now get going."

Peter looked at Andrew and shrugged. Then the two of them started walking double-time to Bethany. "Foal?" Peter thought, "what the heck does he want with a foal? We don't need it to carry anything—we have Philip for that!" He grinned at the thought of Philip, built like a Greek wrestler. So what did Jesus want with a foal? A donkey's foal at that? Jesus usually liked to travel light, and once they got to Jerusalem it was only going to hinder them. Peter had expected Judas to make a stink about the cost of stabling such an animal in Jerusalem, but oddly, he seemed so lost in his own thoughts that he hadn't said a word.

"Hey, hurry up," yelled back Andrew. Peter's reveries had slowed him down and he quickened his pace to catch up with his brother.

Peter was winded by the time they reached the first house in Bethany. And sure enough, just as Jesus had predicted, there was a donkey's foal, tethered and chewing a mouthful of hay. Peter started to say, "How did Jesus know—" but he stopped himself.

Life with Jesus wasn't just weird, it was crazy. He didn't know how Jesus knew—in fact he didn't *want* to know. "Too much weirdness already," he thought as he untied the donkey.

"Hey!" said a blacksmith, coming out of his shack a little ways distant, wiping his hands on his apron. "Whatcha' doin' with the foal?"

Andrew stiffened, but blurted out, "The Lord needs it!"

The blacksmith's eyes narrowed as he took the two filthy fishermen in. "Now look, you two. I don't know what's going on here. A young gent in a white gown was here yesterday and asked if I'd watch this foal until someone called 'the Lord' asked for it. Then he just disappeared. You two look too grimy to be angels. I don't know what your game is, but by all means take the foal, it's obviously waiting here for you."

Peter nodded and grabbed the reins. *The normal kind of weird*, he thought as he and Andrew set off back down the road to Bethany.

When they met up with Jesus, he thanked them and petted the foal's nose as if they were old friends. Then with one arm on the donkey's mane, Jesus wordlessly trudged on to Bethany.

Apparently the watchmen at the Jerusalem city gate had seen them coming for some time, because when they got within earshot, they could already hear people singing "Hosanna!" People started to pour out of the gate and gathered around them. Suddenly their little band of thirty or so had swelled to seventy, a hundred…more. Jesus stopped just short of the gate and went to nuzzle the foal.

"What's he doing?" asked Thomas.

"He and the donkey are having a moment," said Peter wearily. He tired of second-guessing what Jesus was up to. He was increasingly annoyed by Jesus' cryptic stories and sullen demeanor. The romance of being a disciple was wearing off fast, and he wondered what his wife and daughter were doing back home.

Whatever business Jesus and the donkey had been discussing was apparently settled, and Jesus walked back to Mary and asked her for a clean tunic. He put it on and then amid the cheering mob, he swung his leg up and sat up on the foal.

"Um…Lord, what are you doing?" Peter asked impatiently.

"Making my entrance. Get out of the way."

Peter gulped and stood aside. The next few moments were just a surreal blur in his memory. People tore branches from the palm trees, they tore off their coats and, just as Jesus rode through the City gate, they paved his way with them and sang at him.

Peter felt faint and had to sit down, as he was overcome with feelings. "Oh, dear," he thought, "this is going to make a lot of people very upset."

Looking at the Roman guards, he noticed they were yelling at each other, sending messengers tearing off through the streets with the news. Peter knew what they were thinking. Jesus was riding in like a king. Well, except for the donkey part. But the people were certainly acting like he was a King. *Bad news*, he thought, cradling his head. *This, we do not need.*

Next Peter looked at the cheering masses. Jesus' fame had gone before him wherever they went, but this was different. Peter knew what they were thinking. They were thinking that Jesus was the Son of Man. The Son of Man was a popular character in lots of the dime-store apocalypses, the kind of book that a justice-starved population of dreamers just couldn't get enough of. They were cheering wildly and singing, but many of them didn't look comfortable or convinced. Still, the energy of the crowd held sway, and the eerie carnival atmosphere prevailed.

At the rim of the crowd, Peter saw some whispering men, mostly younger. *Zealots*, he thought. They had the same butch haircut that Judas was sporting when he joined up with them. They did not look happy. Nor did the priests and the Pharisees peering down on the crowd from their upper story windows. Peter saw a couple of Sadducees whooping it up, but most were reserved and silent, observing.

Jesus rode placidly, half-smiling at the cheering masses surrounding him. The donkey was spooked, but Jesus held the reins tightly, and the little beast plodded in a reasonably identifiable direction. After a couple of streets of this kind of royal treatment, the crowd thinned out, and Jesus turned the donkey down a sidestreet. Many followed him and crowded around, hoping to touch him or hear a word of wisdom.

Peter shook himself free from his daydreaming and leaped to his feet. Sprinting to Jesus' side, he saw Jesus hand the donkey off to Andrew with some instructions he couldn't hear. Then Jesus spoke briefly to the crowd about keeping a holy passover and bid them good day. He turned and went into one of the houses owned by the Sadducees. Peter followed him.

"Where are you going?" Peter asked.

"This is the guest house for the high priests. I'm going to rest a bit." Peter looked confused.

"They'll toss you into the street!" Peter said, "Are you crazy?"

"My uncle was high priest for fifty years," Jesus answered. "He's only been dead for ten. I will be welcome here. You go on with Mary and the others. She knows where she's going. There's lots to get ready."

"I'm not going anywhere until I get some answers," Peter said defiantly. His voiced cracked, betraying how scared he was to actually face Jesus down like this. Jesus turned and gave Peter his full attention. "Peter," he started, "I'm tired...."

"I want to know just what kind of circus act you were trying to pull out there!" Peter said. His voice wasn't cracking now that his anger was kicking in. "Things aren't bad enough as it is, you have to go and pull a stunt like that?? What were you thinking, Jesus?? Did you get sunstroke? Did the sight of those crosses unhinge your head? What were you thinking??"

Jesus signaled for Peter to follow him up the stairs. He turned in at a small room and sat down. "Put yourself in my place, Peter. What do you think I was thinking?"

"If I had a clue, I wouldn't be standing here imposing myself on your nap time."

Jesus noted the way Peter turned bright red from the neck up. You could almost draw a line around the base of his neck where the redness started. Plus there were two huge veins that popped out of his forehead. Jesus always had to suppress a smile when Peter was mad. Just then he thought, *Those veins stick out so far you could rest a goblet on his forehead*, and then of course he grinned.

"What is so blasted funny?" Peter raised his voice. "You just pulled a very dangerous publicity stunt, and you're already in enough hot water to lose your head. I want to know what is so funny."

Jesus thought about telling Peter that he could rent his forehead out for a pantry but decided against it. "Tell me," Jesus said, "what do you think those people out there were looking for when I came through those gates?"

"Do you always have to answer a question with a question?" asked Peter.

"Do you?" asked Jesus.

"There were lots of people, Lord," Peter started. "They all wanted different things."

"Go on."

"Well, the Romans thought that a really popular rabbi was coming into town."

"Isn't that what happened?"

"Yes, but you came in like some kind of farcical royal procession. If they want an excuse to blame us for sedition, you just gave it to them!"

"I did not pretend to be the Roman emperor."

"That's not the point," Peter shot back. "You intentionally made fun of the emperor."

"I did no such thing." Jesus knelt and started arranging blankets on a mat in the corner.

"Okay, what about the people cheering you on?"

"What about them?"

"They were looking for the Son of Man."

"And they have found him."

"They expected the Son of Man to ride out of the sky and defeat their enemies, like in those cheesy Apocalypses people are always reading nowadays."

"That is a poetic but accurate description," he said passively. "I am the Son of Man, and you could say I 'came from the sky' thirty..." he counted on his fingers "...thirty-three years ago. And as for defeating their enemies, in a week's time I will have done that, too."

"You're going to defeat the Romans in one week?" Peter asked incredulously.

Jesus stood up and narrowed his eyes. "Rome is nothing," he said. "Our biggest enemy is not Rome."

This only made Peter madder. "What about the zealots— some of them support you, you know. If you wanted to score points with them, you should've had your angel or whatever he was deliver a war horse—then they would have proclaimed you king and rallied around you as their leader. Did you have a donkey delivered just to frustrate them?"

Jesus grinned ear to ear. "Yes," he said, "I thought that was a nice touch."

"You don't care, do you?" Peter was shouting now. "You don't give two shakes about making friends, do you? You're a virtual enemy factory, that's what you are! Are you trying to upset everybody in the whole city? Promise them the world and then give them what they do not want?"

"Sit down, Peter, before you break something." Peter did what he was told and Jesus continued. "Tell me, Peter, are you so sure that those people did not get what they wanted?"

Peter thought about it. He put all his questioning and anger on hold for a moment and thought about it. Hard. Jesus waited for a while and then started to rock to the sound of a lyre being plucked out on the street. Finally Peter broke his reverie. "No. I guess you're right. They all got exactly what they wanted, but not in the way that they expected. That's the point, isn't it? We all get what we want, but not the way we want it."

Jesus grinned noncommittally. Then he started to pull off his tunic and get ready for his nap. "And what about you, Peter? What is it you want?"

Peter started to seethe again. "What do you care? What do you care what I want? You break up a good business, you take me away from my family, you make us trudge all over Judea living like paupers, and then you go and pull a stupid stunt like this that's going to get you killed! I don't have any hope of getting what I want. I know what I am getting, though—an ulcer!"

"And you're giving me a headache," Jesus said. He laid down and put a towel over his eyes. "You didn't answer my question. What do you want?"

Peter choked back the emotion that had begun swelling in his throat. "I want you to live. I want you to *live.*"

Jesus exhaled deeply. "You will have what you want, Peter. But not the way you want it."

The Last Testament of Thomas

I don't want to disturb you. But…are you awake? I'm having trouble sleeping, too. Do you mind if we talk? I'm going to die tomorrow…when the sun rises. So I guess I'm a bit restless. It occurred to me, while I was lying here, that when I… when they…when morning comes, no one here will have heard my story. If it's not too much to ask, I mean, if you're not sleeping anyway…will you witness my testament?

My name is Judas. Where I come from, it's not really a very original name. Half of the men in my village were named Judas. It just means "Jewish," you know. And that is what I am—a Hebrew, and far from home.

How did I come to be in an Indian prison? You don't have to ask, I can see it in your face—and not an uncommon question for a foreigner in Indian prisons, I can assure you.

My name is Judas, but nobody calls me that. My nickname is Thomas, which means "twin" in my own language. I am the twin. No, don't ask, "Whose twin?" I'll tell you. I *have* to tell you. Because my story, on its own, is very small. *His* story, though… his story is great. My story is only important because it's part of his.

My brother's name is Y'shua. It's hard to say in your language. Here, we'd call him Jesus. He was born a whole eight minutes before I was. It might as well have been eight centuries, though, when you think about the differences between us. I followed him out of our mother grudgingly, and if I'm honest, I have to admit that I've been following him grudgingly ever since!

Jesus loved to tell stories. And people loved to tell stories about him. Some people say that he was born of a virgin. Someone said that in our mother's presence once and she spit wine out of her nose. If he *were* born of a virgin, my mother didn't know anything about it. And I'm not sure what that would say about *me*. Twin boys, born of a virgin, one of them divine, and the other...just clumsy, I suppose.

People always talk about how full of love Jesus is. He *did* get better at that as an adult, but as a child, he was actually pretty touchy. One time, I remember we were out in the street, and one of the kids in the neighborhood...Levi? Yes, that was his name, Levi. Anyway, he wasn't looking where he was going and he plowed right into Jesus, almost knocked him over. And he didn't stop to apologize, either. Levi just kept right on going.

I was close enough to Jesus to hear him mutter under his breath, "You'll never get where you're going."[1] And sure enough, before the child had taken half a dozen steps, he fell face first into the dust and just...laid there.

I never teased him after that. Or crossed him. Or said "boo" to him, really. He could be intimidating, but he could surprise you, too. Once I remember we were playing in the mud, where this little stream passed just north of our village. I was making matzo balls out of the mud. Jesus teased me for doing "women's work," so I asked him what he was making with *his* mud.

"Sparrows," he said.

"Sparrows?" I asked. "Why not ravens or swallows?" I mean, how much detail can you work into wet mud? I couldn't tell much difference between the lumps of mud he was forming and my matzoh balls, after all.

"Sparrows," he said, and in a few minutes, he had twelve of them, baking in the sun in a row.

"They look an awful lot like matzo balls," I said, and he gave me that dark look which always scared me. So I said no more.

Just then I noticed one of the leaders at the synagogue—ah, that's what we call our local temples—he was standing some distance from us and...glaring at us. Jesus noticed, too, and glared back defiantly.

The man turned on his heel, and I guess he went directly to our father, because in a few minutes, Father came straight for us, walking as fast as it is permissible to walk on the Sabbath.

He did *not* look happy. He pointed to my matzo balls and the twelve lumps at Jesus' feet and demanded, "You know the Law. We are forbidden to make things on the Sabbath. What are you two doing?"

According to our religion, the Sabbath is a day of rest, and if you make something, or walk too much, it is a crime before God. Don't laugh, it's a good religion that way. It is easy to love a God who wants you to rest now and then.

"I'm sorry, Abba," I said.

I thought that Jesus would apologize, too, because we rarely saw Joseph so angry. But he didn't. Instead, he clapped his hands, and those twelve little lumps of mud—would you believe they started fluttering and took to the air?

"Go!" Jesus shouted at them, and they swooped around Father's head, and then they flew off. They did fly a little lumpishly, but they flew. I think Father and I were both a little scared of him after that.[2]

*** *** ***

We weren't the only ones. One time, Zacchaeus, the village tutor, came to Father and said, "Your boy is very clever." He didn't mean *me*, of course. "If you do not educate him, you do him harm."

Father would never want to do anyone any harm, and so after our work for the day, he sent Jesus off to learn his letters. This was a novel thing, so of course I tagged along. I sat on a sack of meal while Zacchaeus and Jesus sat together at the table. Zacchaeus pulled out a scroll and started to recite the letters. "Alef," he said, and waited for Jesus to repeat it.

But Jesus sat with his arms folded across his chest and that scowl on his face. "Repeat after me, Jesus," the teacher said. He was very kind. He pointed to the first letter again, "Alef…"

But Jesus didn't say anything. I saw Zacchaeus' brow furrow in frustration. "Is there something wrong, Jesus?" he asked.

I could see that Jesus was angry, I just couldn't figure out why. I would have leaped at the chance to learn my letters. It seemed to me that Jesus didn't really know why he was angry, either, or… now that I think back on it, perhaps he didn't know how to describe his feelings at that time. Remember that we weren't really educated.

Finally, however, he blurted out, "You're a hypocrite. You say you want to teach me about Alef, but you don't know anything *about* Alef."

Zacchaeus wiped his forehead with the back of his hand, and I could see that he was struggling to control his temper. From everything I had ever heard, he was a sincere and pious man. "Well, Jesus," he said with a little too much patience in his voice, "why don't *you* tell me about Alef?"

And to the astonishment of both of us, Jesus did. He started by describing what each of the pen strokes of the letter represented. He talked about universal ideals and the original man and so forth. He talked about this letter dancing with another, and how each letter represented three things: above the earth, on the earth and under the earth. I mean, I'm not sure half of what he said made any sense at all, but it was an impressive performance.[3]

And when he finally stopped talking, Zacchaeus looked white as a sheet. Without another word he walked out of his house, and we followed him all the way home, to our house. He knocked on the door of Father's workshop, and Father opened it, looking very surprised. "Zacchaeus, I thought you were teaching Jesus his letters. Is everything all right?"

Zacchaeus said, "Your child has shamed me." He pointed at Jesus, and I saw fear in the old teacher's eyes. Fear and anger.

Father scowled at Jesus. "Shamed you? And how did he do that?" But Zacchaeus was backing away, "Keep him away from me, brother!" He pleaded, "I cannot endure his eye! I cannot make sense of his speech! This child is not of this world. This child could tame fire!" And then he turned and ran. I felt a chill go through me, because I knew that Zacchaeus was a terrible gossip. If he was frightened of Jesus tonight, the whole village would be terrified of him by tomorrow.

Father stood blinking in the alley as he watched Zacchaeus retreat. Then, turning his gaze to us, he threw open the door. "Inside," he commanded.

We could see that he was angry, but Jesus wasn't in the mood to apologize. "If you want me to learn, you should send me to someone smart," he said.

"Maybe what you need to learn is respect for your elders," Father said. Father was working on a bed, and I could see that one of the posts had broken where Father had tried to shape it. I realized then that he was already irritated when Zacchaeus had knocked on his door. The wood was not cooperating with him today.

And then something truly amazing happened—and I wouldn't have believed it if I hadn't seen it with my own eyes. Jesus laid one hand on top of the broken post and pulled on it, and he pulled it *up*.[4] It was like the wood stretched several inches, until it was tall enough to shape again and still be as tall as the other posts.

Jesus looked at Father apologetically, but Father only pointed his finger at him. "You're not getting away with it that easily," he said.

*** *** ***

That was just one afternoon, but it was often like that. Jesus just…
rubbed people the wrong way, and other people seemed to rub
him wrong as well. He was often dismissive of me, but he was
never really *mean*. It was like…I just wasn't that important. And
it's true, I suppose, I'm not!

I guess, if I'm honest, I'd have to say that I *loved* my brother,
but I didn't really *like* him. Not back then, anyway. I was *amazed*
by him, I looked up to him, I was jealous of him, but *like* him?
No. He was too…unpredictable, too volatile. I wanted my world
to be safe, and it just *wasn't* safe, not when he was around. Trouble followed him around like a stray cat, and I have *never* sought
out trouble.

But even Jesus had his limits when it came to trouble. I remember when he was about seven or eight, I guess it was, he had
gained a bit of a reputation in the village by that time for precisely the sort of behavior I've been telling you about. The neighbors
had grown wary of him, and some of them even crossed the village square to stay clear of him.

Jesus was playing on the roof of our friend Zeno's house. Apparently Zeno had gotten carelessly close to the edge of the roof,
because he lost his balance and fell into the street.

I was in the doorway of Father's workshop when I saw Zeno's
body hit the dust. I ran toward it as fast as I could, and found
him lying completely still. His eyes were open, and his neck was
twisted at an impossible angle. In moments, there was a whole
crowd around him. We all looked up at roughly the same time to
see where he had fallen from.

And there, peering over the lip of the roof, was Jesus. Of
course, neighbors started yelling that Jesus had pushed him, that
Jesus was a wicked, evil child that ought to be locked up or handed over to the Romans.

The shouts brought my parents out into the street. My mother screamed when she saw Zeno. Father followed the gaze of

the neighbors to the roof, to the offender...to Jesus. Then Zeno's parents came running, and it was total chaos. Zeno's father started screaming at our father, and Father had to put his hands up to ward off the blows. Zeno's father picked up a rock, and I screamed for Father.

I had never been so frightened as I was at that moment. But just then a loud whistle cut through the din and stopped everyone in their tracks. We all looked around, and the whistle came again. This time we looked up. There was Jesus, sitting on the roof with his legs hanging over the side.

"Zeno!" Jesus called. "Hey, Zeno! Get up!" Out of the corner of my eye I caught a stirring near my feet. I stepped back as I saw Zeno's head come round right. Then he pushed himself onto his hands and knees and finally stood up.

"Hey, Zeno," Jesus called again. Zeno looked up. "Zeno, did I push you off the roof?"

Zeno looked confused. "Of course not! I was reaching for a bird, and I fell." Zeno's father dropped the rock, which had been poised about six inches from Father's face. Zeno's mother ran to him and embraced him, covering him in her tears.[5]

After that, Zeno was his best friend—that is, until he fell into a well when he was fifteen or so. Unfortunately Jesus wasn't around to blame *or* to help, that time. So no one could blame Jesus for hurting Zeno, but they were plenty spooked by Zeno's quick recovery from such a...significant accident. It gained Jesus no friends, that's for sure. In fact, I'd say that except for Zeno, Jesus didn't really have any.

Oh, I mean, our brother James and I, we played with Jesus, or we tried to. We tried to be good brothers. But it wasn't easy. If I had to take my pick between Jesus and Zeno, I'd have taken Zeno any day. Zeno was carefree, reckless, and silly, while Jesus was serious, even when he was trying to have fun. Playing with him always felt a little too much like doing chores.

*** *** ***

Zeno wasn't the only child Jesus raised to life again. One morning, James, our youngest brother at the time, was out gathering firewood. When he bent down to pick up a stick, a snake burst out of its den and bit him on the hand.

James dropped all of the wood he was carrying, of course, and ran back to the house, crying. But he didn't make it. He got as far as the village well and then collapsed. People saw him, thank heaven, and ran for Father.

We all rushed to the well, and when we got there we saw James, lying in the street, his head cradled in old Dede's lap. His arm was a blistering red, and had swollen up to the size of a grown man's thigh.

Father knelt and felt at his forehead. Then he put his ear to his mouth, and then he lowered his head to James' chest and began to sob.

I'd never seen Father cry before. I felt confused and frightened and horribly, horribly sad. James was my favorite brother, after all. He was dear, he was noble…at least he didn't frighten me.

When I looked over at Jesus, I saw that he was crying. Jesus knelt next to father, took James' swollen arm in his hands, and lowering his head, he breathed on it.

I swear to you that this is true: James' arm just *deflated*, like a bladder filled with air that has been suddenly punctured. It turned from red to pink, and a moment later, James opened his eyes. He saw Father and Jesus, and he smiled. Do you know what he said? He said, "How is the snake?"

I love my brother James, but I felt love for Jesus in that moment, too. As much as he vexed me, in that moment, he had redeemed himself. I never really *trusted* Jesus, he was too unpredictable, too capricious.

But for the first time—maybe the only time for a very long

time afterwards, too—I thought I might like to be *like* him. I wanted to breathe on people and bring them back to life.

*** *** ***

I'm sorry…I am reminiscing. What is really important to know about Jesus isn't anything that happened when we were growing up, not really. What matters is what happened when he started teaching.

Now, you might say, "A teacher, eh?"…and you are right to be skeptical. I certainly was, given how he acted as a boy.

And I didn't see that changing. One day Jesus was at home, working in the shop alongside me and our other brothers. And the next day, he just took off. We found out later that he'd gone to visit our cousin John. So, that was trouble.

John's father was a priest at the temple in Jerusalem, and everyone thought that John would follow in his footsteps. But no. John had turned his back on his father, and on the whole temple establishment, and went off to study with the Essenes.

Everyone knows *they're* crazy, and now apparently John was, too. He didn't stay with them long, but instead struck out on his own, dressing like Elijah and baptizing people in the Jordan. Uh…baptizing is kind of like ablutions—it is a sign of cleansing, cleansing the soul or…at least one's intentions.

I wasn't there, but friends say Jesus went to John and got baptized. And something happened when he got baptized. Something…profound.

Some people said they heard a voice from heaven, some said they heard thunder, and others say that Jesus just stood there in the water, looking up at the sky, as if he was hearing and seeing something no one else was.[6]

And then he just…disappeared. No one heard from him for a couple of months, and then suddenly we started hearing rumors that he was teaching, as if he were a prophet or something. And he was drawing crowds.

Our neighbor Jacob was the first to hear him. He was away and came across a bunch of people sitting on the ground in the shade, and there was Jesus speaking to them.

Of course we were flummoxed at this news, because Jesus had never shown any interest in being a teacher before. He was a loner, he read a lot, and he was a very complicated kind of person. Not very many people liked him, and he didn't go out of his way to be liked.

"What is he teaching about?" My mother asked him.

Jacob leaned in close so that no one could hear him. "He's teaching about the Kingdom of God."

"Oh, no," my mother said, and I could see the worry on her face.

You see, in our country, there's only one King—Caesar, and only one kingdom—Rome. To talk about the Kingdom of God is treason. If anyone heard him talking about that…well, it could spell trouble.

"It's true," Jacob said, "and I didn't understand a word of it." He looked at my mother with great pity then, and said, "I'm sorry, Mary, but I think the boy is out of his mind."

So of course, we had to go and see for ourselves.[7] We asked around and found him in a nearby village, preaching to a growing group of people. A woman recognized us, and as we came within hearing distance, she announced us to him. "Jesus," the woman said, "your mother and brothers are here." Do you know what he said? He said, "Who are my mother and brothers?"

My mother stopped as if she had been slapped. I came up behind her and put my arm around her to steady her. Jesus ignored us and, gesturing to the people sitting around his feet, hanging on every word, said, "*These* are my mother and brothers—those who do the will of God!"[8]

I looked at my mother's face. She was white as a sheet. Look, I know my brother. I know how he is. But nothing could have prepared me for what he said next. Looking straight at my mother, he said, "If you do not hate your father and mother as I do, you cannot become my disciple. And whoever does not love their father and mother as I do cannot become my disciple. For my mother gave birth to my body, but my *true* mother gave me life."[9]

My mother turned on her heel and went straight home. I wanted to slug him. It wasn't the first time. It wouldn't be the last, either. Mother, my brothers, and I walked home after that. No one said a word.

It wasn't until we were sitting down for the evening meal that my mother could speak of it. "Jacob is right," she said. "He is mad."

I looked at my brothers James and Joseph, and my sister Salome, but none of us contradicted her. Mostly we just stared into our soup.

"I had such hopes for him," Mother said, and sighed. Mother slipped her hand on top of mine and squeezed it.

Without looking at me she said, "Thomas, you are the closest to him—" That wasn't saying much, but I didn't interrupt her. "—I want you to go with him. Look out for him. Keep him… out of trouble." I thought she was going to say, "Quiet," but that would be hoping for too much, I think.

"When?" I said.

"Tomorrow," she said.

And that is how I became a disciple—spying for my mother, and trying to keep Jesus from saying anything too weird or stupid or inflammatory. I might as well have tried to cage the wind.

***   ***   ***

The next morning, I packed a small bag and set off. It wasn't hard to find him again. He was in the same place, and had apparently just finished his morning teaching. He saw me coming, and with a word to his friends, came down the road to meet me.

"Jesus," I said.

"Thomas," he said. "How is Mother?"

I wanted to say, "After that stunt you pulled yesterday…" but I took a deep breath instead. "She's fine."

"What are you doing here?" he asked.

"I thought my big brother might have something to teach me," I answered.

He laughed. "And when you repeat it all to Mother, maybe she'll learn something, too!"

"I think that's a good wager," I said.

"Well, come and meet my other students," he said with a wink. "You can't spy properly without names and such."

"That's kind of you," I said, settling back into our natural banter.

After a couple of strides he stopped to face me, and placed a hand on my shoulder. The mirth was gone from his face, and he gave me a look that was all sincerity. "Thomas, I'm really glad you're here. I know you are skeptical, but I promise that you are going to see some amazing things. I will give you what eyes have never seen, what hands have not touched, and what has never arisen in the human heart."[10]

If he was going to get honest, I decided to do the same. "I'm angry at you," I said. "Your words yesterday hurt Mother terribly."

"Then she didn't really hear me," he said. "Did you?"

I mean, I heard him all right. I had been shocked by his words, too. But I took him to mean, "Did you understand me?" But that was a tall order.

Jesus was forever saying crazy, nonsensical things. Over the next several months I lived with him and his other students as we traveled from village to village. I liked his students, but I don't think they had any better idea than I did what he was getting at. I mean, he would say things like "Blessed is the lion that is eaten by a human, for that lion will become human. And cursed is the human who is eaten by a lion—but the lion will still become human." I mean, does that make any sense to you?[11]

Another time he said, "I am the light which is above all things. I am the All, from me all things have emerged and to me all things have been revealed. Split the wood, and I am there. Lift the stone, and you will find me there."[12]

What could this mean? I mean, my brother is just my brother! We were born at the same time, from the same woman! How is he "above all things"? He always acted like he was the center of the world, as if all things existed for his pleasure. But how have "all things" emerged from him?

I have split wood, and I have not found any self-appointed rabbis even vaguely resembling my brother hiding inside! I began to suspect that old Jacob was right. He *was* mad.

I finally decided to confront him with his nonsense. One evening after supper I took him aside and said, "These teachings of yours are absurd! And since no one can understand them, you're just fostering contempt. How can you expect us to preach such things, too, when we don't understand them ourselves?"[13]

If I'd said something like that to him a couple of years earlier, he would have gone off by himself and sulked. But I think that John's baptism might have actually *done* something to him, because despite my directness—my harshness, even—he responded kindly. He *had* changed. He put his hand on my shoulder and said, "Be patient. It will all make sense."

Except that it didn't. A few days later, we were walking by the lake at Capernaum, discussing spiritual practices. I should say that *we*, the followers, were talking. Jesus might have been listening, but he didn't weigh in until Levi asked him directly, "Do you want us to fast?"

Jesus called over his shoulder, "If you try to fast, you will only sin. Better not."

So then John piped up, "Well, then how should we pray?"

Jesus shot back, "If you pray, others will call you a hypocrite. Better not."

We were all confused by now, so I asked, "Should we give alms?"

To which Jesus responded, "If you give alms, you will give rise to evil within you. Better not."[14]

Exasperated, Judas Iscariot stopped walking and stood with his hands on his hips. "Well then, what foods should we abstain from?"

Jesus stopped too, and looked around at our faces, as if seeing our consternation for the first time. His face softened and he spoke gently, as if explaining to children. "My friends, it isn't what goes into your mouths that will make you unclean, only what comes *out* of them. So when you go out to preach, you should eat whatever people put in front of you, no matter what it is. What is important isn't what you eat, but only that you proclaim the Kingdom and heal the sick."[15]

It was obvious that we were all shocked, and several of the disciples were grumbling. "This message is harsh," they said. "Who can stand to hear it?"[16] This just didn't sound like our religion to us!

"Listen," Jesus said, putting a comforting arm around Judas, who seemed ready to explode, "I'll give you a simple rule you can follow. It will never steer you wrong. Are you ready? Here it is: Do not do what you hate. Because God will always know. Doing what you hate in your heart is a terrible evil. And you can't hide anything from God."[17]

That was the last straw for several of our number. The next morning, as Jesus came back from praying, our numbers were smaller. "Where is Naphtali? Where is Judah?" he asked.

"Can't you guess?" I asked him. "You abuse us with your crazy talk, and then you're surprised when people turn away and go back to sensible lives?"

Jesus looked down at his feet. For the first time since I joined up with his little band, he seemed at a loss. Even as a child, he was always extraordinarily sure of himself, so it was unsettling to see him this way. He shook his head. "Brother," he said, "when John baptized me, the heavens parted and I saw the way the world actually is. And I'm trying to describe that to you all in the simplest way possible. I know it's not making sense yet, but it will. Please…be patient and trust me."

I wasn't sure what to say. I didn't believe him, not really. I mean, I knew that he was an extraordinary person, but lots of people who are mad are the same. Their madness is just…part of their greatness, in a way. Jesus was like that.

"Here is how it is," Jesus said, taking my arm, and walking me to where the others were standing. "If you are seeking, keep on seeking until you find." John overheard, and followed us with his gaze. He was nodding. Jesus continued. "But listen, *when* you find, you are going to become troubled. But don't give up, because your disturbance will give way to amazement. And then…" He dropped my arm and addressed all of us with a grand sweeping gesture, "you will rule over all things, just as I do."[18]

"But I don't want to rule," said Philip.

"Speak for yourself," snapped Judas, and everyone laughed.

Jesus said, "This is exactly what I mean. You're objecting to things to which there is no objection, if only you understood the way things *are*. When you see the world as I do, everything I am saying will make perfect sense."

"But how can we see the world as you do?" John asked, still clearly struggling.

"If you drink out of my mouth, you will become like me," Jesus answered him, almost tenderly. "I also will be as you are, and that which is hidden from you will be revealed."[19]

"Drink from your mouth?" Judas made a face.

"I think he means 'Learn from my words,'" I said. "He's speaking in symbols."

"Of course I am," Jesus said, smiling at me. He touched me on the shoulder, almost dancing. "Truth cannot come into the world naked, it can only be communicated through symbols. People cannot receive it in any other way."[20]

"How can we connect the…symbol…with the thing itself?" John asked.

"Only by means of the symbol can you see the thing itself," Jesus answered. "The truth is that the thing itself is right in front of your face, but because you aren't looking for it, you cannot see it."

John looked down, scowling. Jesus stepped over to him and lifted his chin.

"You are *so* close," he said tenderly. "If you could only see what is before your face, everything else would be revealed to you, too."[21]

For a fleeting moment, he seemed to be making sense. And for a moment, I had the fleeting, frightened thought: What if he isn't mad? What if he really *can* see something that none of the rest of us can see?

As soon as I had that thought, the knot in the thick of my belly loosened. I relaxed. Instead of being edgy and suspicious, I became…curious. Instead of being concerned for Jesus and at the same time angry at him, I began to wonder at him.

For the first time, he seemed to me somehow more than the self-absorbed twin brother that made my life miserable. I found that, for the first time in my life, I was *enjoying* his company.

I mean, yes, I get it. Jesus was the elder brother—by eight minutes, but still—he *had* to be first. He had to be the center of attention, he needed my attention and my loyalty and my service. None of that had changed. But for some reason, in that moment, I didn't *resent* it.

Instead, it seemed right, it seemed reasonable, maybe even necessary. He seemed to promise something just out of sight, just around the corner, something grand, something important, something infinite.

***   ***   ***

My breakthrough came about a week later. We were walking toward Samaria when Nathaniel asked Jesus when the Kingdom would arrive. Everyone's ears pricked up when he asked that, because that really was what everyone wanted to know. I don't mean just us, I mean every person in Judea.

When would God raise up a leader to throw off the yoke of Roman oppression? When would God restore home-rule to Jerusalem? *That* was what "the Kingdom" meant to us, to all of us! It was what everyone had been praying for, for generations. I mean, we had no sooner gained our freedom from Babylon than we were vassals of Persia, then we were conquered by the Greeks, and now the Romans. Our people ached to once again know no king but God alone.

Jesus stroked his chin, as if wondering how much to reveal. Finally, he spoke, but he looked at his hands as he did so. "It's not going to arrive—" There was a collective gasp from everyone around us.

Judas Iscariot looked like a bladder ready to burst. "—not in the way you expect, anyway. It isn't going to come in a way you can see *out here*." He waved around at the road, at the scrub bushes, at the trees. "It isn't going to come in such a way that you'll be able to say, 'Here it is,' or 'There it is, over there!' That's not how it's going to be."[22]

"But that goes against everything we've always been taught," Peter said morosely. He looked defeated.

Jesus nodded. "We've all been taught wrong." For a moment he looked angry, but then a smile broke out across his face. "I mean, listen, if our teachers said, 'Look, the Kingdom is in the sky!' then won't the birds achieve home-rule before you do?"

"But no one is saying, 'The Kingdom is in the sky,'" Judas grumbled.

Jesus ignored him, "And if our teachers said, 'The Kingdom is in the sea,' then the fish will be free before we are."[23]

"No one is saying 'The Kingdom is in the sea!'" Judas snapped.

Jesus gave him an annoyed look. "You're not helping," he said simply.

"Neither are you," Judas shot back.

"I'm speaking figuratively," Jesus said. "The truth can only be delivered through symbols, remember?"

"Seems to me, if it's the truth, you should be able to speak about it plainly, without resorting to nonsense."

For a moment, they just stared at each other. Then Jesus softened. "I'll tell you a story—" he started.

"Oh, here we go…" moaned Judas, and he stormed off.

"We're here," John said. "Tell us the story."

"Sit," Jesus, said, indicating a shady clearing.

Once we'd all gotten settled, he began. "The Kingdom of God is like this woman who had a jar of wheat flour," he started. "She was carrying it from the miller to her home, but she accidentally broke the handle off of the jar. She lifted it up into the hollow above her hip, and balanced it there as she walked home. What she didn't realize, however, was that there was now a hole in the jar from where the handle had broken off. So she trailed flour behind her the whole way home. When she arrived there, she had no flour left, as it had all run out."[24]

He sat back with a satisfied look on his face.

"And that's what the Kingdom of God is like?" Andrew asked.

"Just so," Jesus said, smiling.

"And what, for the love of Gehenna, is that supposed to mean?" Andrew asked a little hotly.

"It's obvious," Jesus said, his face falling.

"Not to us," Peter said, looking a little concerned.

Jesus pursed his lips and then began slowly. "The woman scattered flour all over the road, but she didn't notice it. In the very same way, the Kingdom of God is spread out upon the earth, but most people don't notice it.[25]

"We don't have to wait for the Romans to leave—the Kingdom is already here. The earth *already* belongs to God—Caesar only *thinks* he rules it. The earth is the Lord's, and all that is in it![26] The Kingdom is already here! We are already in it! The Kingdom is inside of us, and it is outside of us. Don't you see?"[27]

And that's when it happened. I looked over the Judean hills, at the setting sun, at the scrub, at the distant land of the Samaritans. And I saw that all of it was God's. We weren't waiting for God's rule—God already ruled it. Rome's rule was a mass delusion.

That revelation instantly led to another: If God is Lord of all that is, then the Kingdom *is* all that is. All that *is*…is God's! And since God is everywhere, all that is is *in* God. Maybe all that is… *is* God.

I felt a cold chill descend down my spine, despite the summer heat. I dared not say a word of this to anyone else, because it was blasphemy. And if I was right, if this was indeed what Jesus was trying to get at, then no wonder he was being so cryptic, so circumspect. Not only was he trying to communicate something that was essentially unsayable in human language, but it was something that could get him stoned by the religious authorities. Or worse.

During the next several days I stumbled around in a disoriented daze. The new reality Jesus was preaching about made my head spin.

It was indeed the Kingdom, and a much grander, much more powerful, much more profound Kingdom than anyone in Israel actually imagined. The implications of it continued to buffet me as I began to get my sea legs in this new world, this new universe. I must have grown quiet because, although he didn't say anything, Jesus was keeping his eye on me.

***　***　***

We stopped to stay the night with our family friend, Lazarus, and his two sisters, Mary and Martha. Jesus was holding forth after supper, of course, saying his typical confounding things. Confounding, that is, if you didn't get what he was talking about.

This new Kingdom I seemed to have shifted into as a result of his teachings must have been right, because now everything he was saying was making sense. Crazy.

Most of us were reclining around the table, while Mary and John sat at Jesus' feet. They were looking just as perplexed as everyone else, the more so the longer Jesus taught. A week ago, my brow would have been just as furrowed as theirs. Now I felt an easy lightness as Jesus' teaching seemed to bring new light into formerly dim corners of my brain.

Jesus was telling us a parable about the Kingdom involving yeast when Martha burst through the door from the kitchen. "Jesus!" she yelled, "I'm in here doing all the work while Mary just lounges at your feet, hanging on every word. Is that fair? Tell her to get moving and help me out here."

Jesus cocked his head and considered her. Do you know what he said? "Martha, you are troubled by many things. But only one thing is important. And Mary is tending to *that*. I'm not going to take that away from her."[28]

It was a good answer, and I thought that was going to be that. But then Peter piped up and said, "Martha is right. It's not proper for women to study Torah. Mary should not be here."

Everyone looked to Jesus, then all eyes shifted to Lazarus, who was hosting this little party. Lazarus looked like a frightened newt, saying nothing. Everyone looked back to Jesus.

"Well, then," Jesus said. "I guess I'll just have to make her an official male." He grinned broadly, and reached out to pat Mary, which I took to mean "you stay right where you are."

But then he turned serious, and said, "Don't you worry, Peter. I will lead Mary, and I will make her male so that she will be the equal of you males. For any woman who makes herself male will enter the Kingdom...."[29] He stopped mid-sentence, his voice rising as if he were going to say something else, but he didn't. Instead, he looked around the room, as if looking for someone who understood what he was saying, for someone to finish his sentence.

I did understand, to my great amazement, and so I obliged him. "...And any man who makes himself female will likewise enter the Kingdom," I said, my voice oddly resonant and sounding a little too loud in that tiny room. I realized that everyone was looking at me, but I fixed my eyes on my brother's face alone.

He took a bite of bread, but he was looking right into my eyes, and his smile broadened as he chewed. "Thomas has the whole of it," he said, after he swallowed.

"H-h-how can I become a female?" Peter spluttered. "What can this possibly mean? Are these more symbols?"

Jesus shook his head. "No, this is plain speaking. And when you enter the Kingdom—" he looked in my eyes again, grinning, "—you'll understand exactly what I mean. Shall I speak even plainer?" Heads nodded all around. "Very well, then," he said. "When you make the two into one, and the inside like the outside, and the outside like the inside, and the top like the bottom, and when you make the male and the female into a single one, so that the male is not male and the female is not female, then, and only then, will you will enter the Kingdom."[30]

Jesus locked eyes with me, and I nodded. He nodded. Outside of the womb, it may have been the most intimate moment my twin and I had ever shared.

*** *** ***

The next day, we had taken leave of our hosts and were heading toward another village about two days' journey. As we walked, the other Judas—Iscariot that is—started to question Jesus about his authority.

"Why should people listen to your bizarre interpretations of the Law?" Judas asked. "You're not even a proper rabbi."

"And yet, here you are, listening to me," Jesus said. He smiled at Judas, but the smile looked forced. In my opinion, my once-impatient brother was being far too patient. Or perhaps it was simply that my own perspective had changed. Not long before, I would have been hanging on every word of this exchange, just hoping for the opportunity to hear Jesus hang himself with his own rope. *Authority indeed*, I would have thought. But now...

At some point, Jesus' frustration began to show. He stopped us in the shade of a fig tree and sat down, wiping sweat from his forehead. "Look, my friends, it doesn't matter what I say about my right to teach. What matters is what you think about me." He turned to Peter and said, "Peter, people value your opinion. Who do you say that I am?"

Peter looked around uncertainly. "You are Jesus bar Joseph, from Nazareth. Is this a trick question?"

"No, no," Jesus assured him. Irritation flashed on his face, but he controlled it. "Let's try this: Compare me with something, and tell me what I am *like*."

"Oh, all right," Peter said. Peter chewed on his lip and looked to the hills. Then he looked back at Jesus. "You are like a righteous angel. I think you are a heavenly being, sent here to reveal the mysteries of heaven to us."

Jesus nodded without commitment. Then he turned to Matthew. "Matthew, you're a man of the world. What do you think I am like?"

Matthew didn't need to pause. Immediately he said, "You are like a wise philosopher, a man of extraordinary insight."

Again, Jesus nodded without comment. To my great amazement, Jesus turned next to me. "And what do you say, brother? What do you say I am like?"

My eyes locked on his for a moment, and I could hear the shuffling of feet and the rustle of cloth around me. "Master, I am not capable of describing what you are like. No human mouth can do it."

My words shocked me, for I had never called him "master" before. He was my brother, not my lord. And yet it had been said, and could not be taken back.

But Jesus shook his head, "Thomas, I am not your master. I

am simply the one who showed you the living water." He grinned. "You drank it. And I think you became a little drunk on it."[31]

I grinned back, and another moment of intimacy passed between us. I realized something significant had changed, not just in me, but in our relationship. I mean, I have always loved my brother, but as I said, as children, I never liked him. And as an adult...well, I thought he was crazy, you know, I thought he was sick.

I still loved him, of course, but I didn't respect him, I didn't admire him, I certainly didn't trust him. Pity him? Yes. Resent him? The shame he visited upon the family, and heartache he'd caused mother? Oh, yes, I resented him.

But now those feelings were fading like a dream in the first light of morning. I began to understand why he was the way he was. He didn't intend to be hurtful. If he were going to be honest, there was no other way for him to be. And if he was truly honest, perhaps he was trustworthy too....

Jesus got to his feet and motioned to me, "Come away with me, brother." Peter's eyebrows raised and Judas scowled as Jesus took me aside for a private word. When we were out of earshot, he searched my face. "I think you've seen it."

I nodded. "You know it, Master," I said. The word didn't seem strange the second time I said it. If felt right in my mouth.

"So tell me. Describe it to me in your own words. Tell me what you have seen." I looked back at the other disciples. "Don't worry, they can't hear you," he said. "And you will have no trouble from me, no matter what you say. So just say it, even if it's broken, or partial, or messy. Just say it." He clapped me on the shoulder and squeezed it. "Just *say* it."

I met his eyes and opened my mouth. "Okay then. I think there is only one thing in the universe. And that thing is God."

"Go on," he prompted.

"I think you have seen that...*you* are that thing, too."

"And?" he prompted.

"And so is everything else."

He pulled me toward him until our foreheads touched. "I love you like my own soul," he said. "And I will protect you as the pupil of my own eye."[32]

I embraced him then. I held him for a long time. I suppose, in my heart, I still am.

After Jesus and I returned to the others, they pressed me for details of our conversation. I smiled at them, but just shook my head. "If I told you what we were talking about, you would stone me."

Peter's brow furrowed and he looked agitated. They all did, except for John. He looked curious. I think he was on the verge of "the shift."

"But the real danger wouldn't be to me," I said, "but to you. Because if you stoned me, fire would come out of the rocks in your hands and would *eat you up!*" I lunged at Peter and slapped at the bald spot on the top of his head. He jumped, his eyes wide. Everyone else laughed.

***   ***   ***

About a month later we were in Samaria. We were kind of hiding out, because whenever we set foot in Judea, doctors of the Law and some of the more hard-line Pharisees took the opportunity to threaten Jesus and try to trap him. He was wily, and I often admired the way he danced around their arguments. He rarely placed a wrong step, and he publicly embarrassed *them* more often than the other way around. But things had been heating up, and we were getting worried. Their attacks had become more threatening, more vitriolic. Who knew what they'd try?

One afternoon a messenger from Bethany ran up to us. He caught his breath as we called for Jesus, who was napping. When Jesus joined us, the man handed him a note. As Jesus read it, I watched the blood drain out of his face. He swallowed and handed the note to John, who was standing nearest him.

John said, "It's from Martha. Lazarus is ill. She wants Jesus to come at once."

Peter shook his head. "It's not safe for you to go back to Judea right now. It's not wise."

Jesus seemed to agree, but what he said was, "He's not that sick. God's will be done." And he sent the messenger on his way.

For two days more, we continued as if nothing had happened. But Jesus seemed distracted, disturbed. Two days later, Jesus woke up looking like he'd seen a ghost. "We've got to go back to Judea. Lazarus has...fallen asleep."

"That's a bad idea," Judas said. "They'll stone you."

"Besides," said Thaddeus, "If he's just asleep, he'll get better."

"What I mean," Jesus said, a little sadly, "is that Lazarus is dead."

"How do you know this?" Peter asked. "Was there another messenger this morning?"

Jesus shook his head. "No. I just...know."

"He just *knows*," Judas said to Peter sarcastically.

"I need to go to him now," Jesus said, and he started to roll up his blanket.

So I knelt and started rolling up mine. "Maybe we'll all end up in the tomb with Lazarus," I said, "but if Jesus is going, I'm going."

It was an off-the-cuff comment at the time, but it turned out to be disturbingly prescient. We went to Lazarus' grave, and when we got there, he had been dead for three days. He'd died the same morning Jesus had woken up with that...knowing. And to our great amazement, Jesus went into his tomb and led Lazarus out, limping but alive.

That was hard for even me to believe. I mean, yes, I understood that all things are one in God. Good and evil, light and dark, male and female, matter and spirit—but dead and alive, too? Is there no real distinction between *anything*? The answer, it seemed, was no.

*** *** ***

My faith in this new view of the Kingdom would be sorely tested, however, because once back in Judea, Jesus was determined to go to Jerusalem for the Passover—that's our most important feast of the year, the most sacred to our God. The dream for all Jews is to be in Jerusalem for Passover, much as it is for you Hindus to be at the Ganges when you die.

And dying is what he did. It was powerfully dangerous for him to go—and we told him so. Everyone warned him. Those most rigid in their religion wanted blood, and those who were collaborating with our Roman occupiers wanted a scapegoat for all the upheaval and trouble. And the zealots wanted revenge, because Jesus wouldn't take up arms and be the kind of messiah they wanted him to be. Their Kingdom would only come by force of arms and personality, and Jesus would not play those games. So all of these groups found their target in my brother, and they loosed their arrows. How could he hope to escape?

To be honest, I don't think he did. I think he knew exactly what was going to happen, and he walked into it with his eyes wide open. And they arrested him, and they crucified him, and he died.

I didn't see it happen. I mean, we're identical twins! It's not like people didn't know what Jesus looked like—and I was always being mistaken for him. That was one day I did *not* want to be mistaken for him. Besides, I just couldn't watch. He was my brother, after all. I couldn't just stand by and watch it happen. So I didn't.

Of all of us who followed him, only John was there at the last. Mother was there, too. And our aunt Mary, and the other Mary, the wealthy widow from Magdala that Jesus loved. I think they might have married if...

Afterwards, I was a wreck. For thirty years, I'd had this love/ hate relationship with my brother, and then, only at the last, only

in the past few months have I felt like we really *saw* each other…
and then he was gone.

I felt like crawling into that tomb with him.

John took mother home with him. He was wonderful with
her. I visited, but she wouldn't speak to me. She turned her face
away and ignored every word I spoke.

I told her about the Kingdom, about how Jesus and I had truly found each other at the end, but she couldn't hear me. She had
sent me to keep him safe, to keep him out of trouble. I had failed.

It was the end of the road, and we all felt it. Everyone started
to make plans to go home, to take up their old jobs, to go back to
the lives that Jesus had…interrupted.

And then Mary—the widow Jesus would have married—she
returned from Jesus' tomb with a wild story. I wasn't there when
she showed up, but Peter and John both told me about it.

She was babbling like a madwoman, but when she calmed
down enough to speak, she said that when she got to the tomb, it
was empty. They ran to the tomb with her, and it was exactly as
she said.

Mary was upset, of course, wondering who could have stolen
his body, and why. Then the groundskeeper spoke to her, and
then suddenly he wasn't the groundskeeper at all, but Jesus himself, asking her why she was weeping.

"Teacher!" she said and fell at his feet. He told her not to
grasp after him…which I thought was an odd thing to say. I've
thought a lot about that since then, and I don't think he was saying, "Don't touch me." I think he was saying, "Don't hold on to
your old ideas about who I am," or maybe "*what* I am."[33]

Because the shift that I had seen—the shift that I think John
was beginning to see, too—Jesus was…acting it out. He was
making it so clear that none of the others could miss it. There is
no male or female, no insiders or outsiders, no matter or spirit,
no oppressors or victims, no life or death—everything is united,
everything is one.

And the fact that he was both dead and not-dead at the same time? Well, that just proved it, it displayed it, it bore witness to *exactly* what Jesus was trying to teach.

But at the time, I was too heartbroken. Once again, I didn't understand what Jesus was up to, and I thought that Mary's talk about him being alive again was just wishful thinking. Maybe her love for him was so great that when he died, she snapped. I've known it to happen.

It was harder to explain when, several days later, Jesus appeared to all the disciples—all except for me, of course, and the Iscariot, who committed suicide, but that's another story.

Could they *all* have been delusional? I told them I wouldn't believe it unless I could put my fingers in the nail holes in his hand. Not unless I could put my hand in his side, where a soldier's spear had pierced him.

They stepped back in alarm when I said that, and as I look back at it, I think that I threw the ball a bit too far.

I postponed my plans to travel back to Nazareth, mostly out of concern for the others. And then, after supper one evening, as we were discussing what we should do now, Jesus was suddenly *in the room.*

I know this is hard to believe. It was hard for *me* to believe. One moment we were sitting in depressed silence and the next, everyone was talking at once, hugging, back-slapping, jostling one another just to be close to him.

Jesus took this all good-naturedly, of course. After he had greeted everyone else, and the noise had died down, he looked over to where I was sitting.

I know, I know, I should have been in the throng. I should have rushed to him, I should have showered him with kisses. But I was ashamed.

I think this is *always* the way it is. I don't think God has ever pushed anyone away because of what they have done. I think *we turn away* because of our shame.

That is certainly what was happening inside me at that moment. I was too ashamed to cheer him, to greet him, to kiss him. So I sat there until he came to me.

He didn't say anything. He just held up his palm. And I could see the hole that the nail had made, still raw and gory, right through his wrist. He held it there until I reached up and touched that terrible hole.

I swear by all that is holy, he flinched. But he didn't draw it back. He kept it right there, for me to touch, to explore, to violate again.

Tears erupted from my eyes and I cast myself to his feet and found that they, too, were horrible. Pierced. No longer bleeding, but not yet healed, either.

He was solid, but he was also cold, as if it were no longer blood that animated him, but some other unseen, unknowable essence. Some vital unguent no longer susceptible to threats, to betrayal, to tyranny, to illusion or any other evil.

"My lord and my God!" I sobbed, bathing his cold feet with hot tears.[34]

Before I had spent my shame and my sorrow, he lifted me to my feet and embraced me. "Now that you have seen me, brother," he said, "trust me. I really need you to trust me. Because you will touch others who have not seen me. They will trust me because *you* trust me."

I nodded, not really taking it all in. But I knew: everything was changed now. The Kingdom wasn't just a new way of seeing, it was a whole different reality. A reality that, once you beheld it, it *changed* you. And the greatest evidence of that change was holding me in his strong, solid, cold arms.

I mean, the brother I had grown up with was self-obsessed and aloof, but since he had seen the Kingdom—since he realized that he *was* the Kingdom—he had become kind, thoughtful, trustworthy, and wise.

His rising from the dead was shocking, but I would be hard-pressed to say which of the two transformations was more pro-found.

But then I realized that Jesus was speaking again. Every word he said was a clanging, ringing shout of affirmation of every teaching that had seemed so obscure up until now.

There is no heaven, there is no earth. There is no death, there is no life. There is no other, there is no self, there is only this moment, this holding, this confused gush of shame and joy and relief and sobs and the rough cloth twisted in my fist in the small of his back as I hugged him to me.

My brother, my twin, my master, my God, myself…as he held me, all distinction, all separation, all two-ness fell away. "This is the Kingdom," he said. And he breathed on me.

***   ***   ***

Nothing was the same after that. Jesus was the same…but differ-ent. He was always cold, for one thing. His body…it was *his* body, no question, but it *wasn't* his body. It was solid and *not* solid. It was him and *not* him. It wouldn't have made any sense to me if I still thought that difference was real. I don't know how the other disciples were thinking about it. It wasn't something we…talked about.

I talked with Jesus rather a lot, though. I think we talked more in the first month after he…came back to life than in the whole of our lives up 'til then.

His personality was different, too. I mean, it was still *him*, but the ways in which he put people off were…softer. But in other ways, he was more severe. It's hard to explain, but he was more gentle with people, more sensitive to their feelings, but at the same time, he was quicker to confront them with really hard things. But he did it more deftly than before, so that instead of taking offense, people actually seemed grateful.

Soon after he rose from the dead, he started getting up really early. It was like he didn't need sleep anymore, he just did it as a courtesy to us. So once we were all asleep, he would get up and sit by the fire—praying, I imagine.

I joined him long before dawn on many mornings. The times we spent together were some of the most tender moments we ever shared. And the things he said.... One time he said, "Those who weep, those who are oppressed are blessed."[35]

"How do you figure that?" I asked.

"Because the people who oppress them are without hope."[36]

"Wait," I said. "Do you mean that they oppress because they have no hope? Or that they have no hope because they will not escape judgment?" He didn't answer me, of course.

"The oppressed will be released from every form of bondage," he said. "That's God's dream. That's what everything is unfolding toward. The bitterness of this life will pass. Those who toil will find rest. Suffering and disgrace will be left behind. They will reign with God, they will be one with God. This will last forever."[37] He looked over to me and I saw his cold eyes sparkle in the firelight. "I have seen it. I *am* it."

"I still want to know what will happen to the oppressors," I said.

He nodded. "It will be tragic for those who have no hope. They are driven by the fire of desire, and it is insatiable. The burning that is in them will devour them. They suffer because the wheel in their minds constantly turns! They suffer because they are captives, chained in caves."

"What caves?" I laughed. "Let's go rescue them!"

He kept staring at the fire, but I saw him smile. "Don't laugh!" he said. "They don't know they are chained in a cave. They don't know that they are doomed, they don't realize the circumstances they are really in. They don't know that they are living in darkness and death. Instead, they are drunk on the burning of desire. So much so that the very things that wound them seem sweet to them! Everything is upside down—they cling to darkness as if it were light, to slavery as if it were freedom. They think they hold the power...but the fact is they are held by it."[38]

"But I don't understand," I said. "If everything is one in God, then how will the wicked be any worse off than the good?"

He tilted his head from side to side. "You are still thinking of things in terms of two-ness," he said. "Do you remember that time when that man from Hebron approached me and said, 'Master, you must go and speak to my brothers so that they will divide my father's belongings with me fairly'—do you remember that?"

I smiled. "Yes, and you said, 'Mister, who made *me* a divider?'"[39] It was a great joke, because everything you say seems to divide people."

"And yet, you are doing the same. You want me to divide people into 'wicked' or 'good,' and you want justice to be done."

"Isn't that what you're talking about?" I asked. But he shook his head. "Everyone comes to the Father. Everyone receives his light. Those who have cultivated joy will receive that light as infinite joy. Those who have cultivated love will perceive that light as infinite love. Those who have lived only for greed will perceive it as infinite need. Those who have cultivated aggression will perceive it as infinite threat."

He paused for a long moment, then he took a drink from a flagon of wine at his side. "But it is all the same. That is why it is so important to know yourself, to know what drives you, to know the kind of seed you are sowing. You will harvest exactly what you sow.[40]

"Because if you do not know yourself, you know nothing. But if you know yourself," he passed the flagon to me, "well, then you know everything."[41]

"Because I am everything," I said. He didn't answer me. "And because I'm everything, if I hurt another…"

"You hurt everything," he finished.

"And if I hurt myself—"

"You hurt everything." He took the flagon back. "Only the whole is real."

And that is why I don't mind being in prison so much. Inside, outside, it's all the same. The real prisoner is the king and his advisor, who put us here.

Oh, do you think that is impertinent? Ha! You haven't heard anything yet, my friend. There is plenty of impertinence where that came from!

***   ***   ***

At this point you might be thinking, "But how did this poor old Jew get to India?" My brother rising from the dead was an unexpected twist, but in some ways, getting *here* is the most surprising aspect of my journey.

Jesus' return from death recharged us. Far from being defeated and discouraged, we finally understood—no one could oppose us now. Not even death could stop us. I mean, here was Jesus, cold but alive, eating with us, laughing with us—not diminished, but somehow even *more* than he was before. And he promised that same resurrection to us.

The fiercest threat our Roman captors could level against us was the threat of death. And *that* was no longer a threat. It seemed impossible to throw the ball too far. So what to do, where to go?

And then one day at breakfast, Jesus said to us, "There will be times when you will want to hear my voice, and it will seem like I am not here. You will look for me, but you will not see me."[42] Everything went hush, and I could hear the others breathing.

"Don't be afraid. Even if you don't see me, I will be there among you. Especially when two or more of you are together."[43]

I felt tense and I looked away. And when I looked back, he was gone. No one saw him go.

But it's not like he *stayed* gone. He kept showing up at odd times and in unexpected places—and I don't mean that figuratively. I'll tell you what I mean....

After Jesus'...disappearance, we returned to Jerusalem. He

had told us to "go forth and teach all nations," so we thought we'd be efficient about it. We procured a map and then we divided up the world. And then we cast lots to see who should go where. Three guesses which country I got.[44]

Now, I had heard about India. I mean no offense, my friends, but your beloved country has a reputation of being hard. I have never had what I would call a robust constitution. I was always the sickly one in the family, though it pains me to say it. It wasn't that I was unwilling to go and preach, indeed, I would say I was even eager. But I would have preferred to have been sent to some-place more...hospitable to those of precarious health. I mean, I found even the countryside of Judea challenging. But India?

I shuddered at the mere thought of it. So I told the other disciples, "No. I'm willing to go many places, but not there." They thought I was just being difficult. And...maybe I was.

That same night I was alone in my room, trimming the wick of an oil lamp, when Jesus handed me a candle out of the blue. I nearly jumped out of my skin.

"Ready to go to India?" he asked.

"I'm not going to India," I told him.

"Why not?" he asked. There was no use lying to him or dodging the question.

"Because I'm afraid to go to India," I said simply.

"Why are you afraid?" he asked. "What is there to be afraid of?"

"Stomach cramps and the runs?" I suggested.

He laughed. "Yes, you will get those," he said.

"Are you saying that to comfort me?" I asked. "If so, you're doing a terrible job."

"Brother," he put a cold hand on my arm, "if you refuse, how will the others feel? You need to set a good example."

My shoulders sank when he said that. I knew it was true.

"Don't be afraid," he said. "Go and proclaim Good News to the people in India. They need some."

"Send me anywhere else," I protested, "anywhere but there."

But when I looked over at him, he wasn't there. *Again*. I cursed and threw his candle across the room.

*** *** ***

The next day, around lunchtime I think it was, I was at the market place. And suddenly Jesus was there again. I didn't recognize him at first, because he had changed his appearance. He was dressed as a merchant, and he was clean-shaven.

"Come with me," he said. I shrugged and set off after him. He led me to another merchant, one wearing what looked like very exotic garb to me at the time. Jesus spoke to the man, saying, "Here, Abbanes, this is Judas." He didn't say, "Judas my brother," or "Judas my twin," as he usually did, and that should have tipped me off that something was amiss right there.

Abbanes looked me up and down as if he were examining a bolt of cloth. After what seemed like far too long, he finally looked me in the face. I thought he was going to examine my teeth, but instead he afforded me the dignity of being acknowledged and spoken to.

"Judas, is it?"

"Yes," I said. "That is my name. Although most people call me Thomas. That means—"

But he interrupted me. "Tell me, Judas, is this man your master?" he pointed at Jesus.

I gave Jesus a quizzical look, but I answered the man. "Yes… he is my master," I said.

"And you are a carpenter," he said.

I wasn't sure if it was a question or a statement, but I replied, "I am."

"Are you a good carpenter?" he asked.

"Our father was the best carpenter in Nazareth, and he taught us well," I said, looking at Jesus with daggers in my eyes. He was looking at his sandals and whistling softly.

"Good," the man said, and clapped me on the back. "I have just purchased you. You are now in the service of King Gundaphorus."

I glared at Jesus, but he refused to look at me. "You have *purchased* me?" I asked.

"Yes, from your master. Come along. We sail at the fourteenth hour."

Never taking my eyes from Jesus, I asked him, more than a little testily, "And where do we sail to?"

"To India, of course," the man said.

I looked at the merchant now. I saw that he was well-dressed, but small of stature. His skin was dark, his hair was oiled. He looked kind. I took some comfort in that. "May I...speak to my... former master privately before we go? We have been...close. I would like to say goodbye."

He gave leave, but admonished me to be quick. Taking Jesus aside, I whispered through clenched teeth, "That was snake-belly low, even for you. I've seen you do some pretty shameful things, brother, but this—"

He ignored me. And placed a money purse in my hand.

"What's this?" I demanded.

"This is the money that I got for you."

I poured the contents into my hand.

"Twenty pieces of silver? That's it? That's insulting. Iscariot sold *you* for thirty."

Jesus closed my hand around the coins. "I wish it were more, too, but it will suffice. I promise." He pushed our heads together, an intimacy I did *not* crave at that moment.[45]

"Thomas," he whispered. "I know this is hard...but to be close to me is to be close to the fire."

"So I see," I said. "And to be far from you? I am headed off to the far East, it seems."

"To be far from me is to be far from the Kingdom.[46] Which... is not an option for you now. You have seen too much."

And then he kissed me, and then he was gone. *Again.* Just like that. Probably a good thing, or I might have strangled his cold neck until it was...I don't know, *colder*, I suppose. I could hardly see straight, I was so angry. I felt tricked, I felt betrayed. To be honest, I felt like killing him...but I've seen how *that* turns out.

*** *** ***

So we set sail. I helped out at sea, doing carpentry work. The tools were odd and some were unfamiliar, but I warmed to them quickly enough.

I found the sea frightening at first, but then exhilarating, and after several weeks had passed, almost unremittingly dull. So I was not sad when we finally pulled into port in the kingdom ruled by Gundaphorus.

Once ashore, Abbanes led me directly to the palace. We waited in an enormous, vaulted chamber, the likes of which I had never seen, and despite my fears, I could not help myself—I pored over the wood, fascinated by the novelty of its construction, its beauty, its genius.

Finally, however, we were summoned into the presence of the King. As we knelt before him, Gundaphorus looked me over critically, one black brow sunk low over a baggy eye in scrutiny.

Given leave to speak, Abbanes introduced me, and the King commanded me to rise. "You are a Hebrew, then?" he asked.

"I am," I replied.

"And you are a carpenter?"

"My whole life, sir," I said, keeping my eyes on his feet.

"What skills do you have in wood, and what skills in stone?" the King questioned.

I should have been shaking in my sandals, but instead I felt calm and at peace. I felt a familiar arm on my shoulder, but when I looked at Abbanes, it wasn't his. The arm was cold.

I smiled and answered the King. "I am skilled with ploughs, yokes, goads, pulleys, and now boats and oars and masts. As for stone, I can construct pillars, temples and court-houses for kings, your majesty." I gave a little bow.

The king smiled as well, apparently pleased at my answer, or at least at the *way* I answered. "Tell me, Hebrew, can you build me a palace?"

I had never built anything more than a single-story stone dwelling for peasants back home. The construction of just his antechamber confounded and amazed me. How could I possibly create something as grand, or *more* grand? I was well out of my depth.

But then a familiar voice whispered in my ear. "I can," it said.

"I can," I repeated. "I can both build it and furnish it. That is why I am here."

*** *** ***

The next few days were a whirlwind, as I accompanied the King to the site of the new palace. As we walked, we discussed the best methods of laying foundations, of different methods of cutting and laying stone.

When we reached the site, Gundaphorus showed me where the court-house should be, where the grand hall was to be located, where the servants quarters would go. A servant took measurements, and a scribe wrote them down.

I nodded my approval. "This is a fine site," I told him, trying to sound authoritative. But the truth was, I was terrified and had no idea what I was doing. I would need several months to study the architecture and methods of my new home if I didn't want to bungle this up horribly.

"*But*," I said, "it is also marshy and wet. We should wait until winter to begin."

The King scowled at me. "If you think it is wet now, the monsoons will come in a few months—this is nothing. Most carpenters would want to get to work immediately."

I didn't know what a monsoon was, but I desperately needed the time.

"Are you sure you want to begin in the winter?" he asked.

"It cannot be done any other way," I said, which was the truth, although not in the way he heard it.

"Very well," the King said, still looking unsure. "Begin to draw up some plans. I must go abroad for a year or so, but when I return, I expect to see my new palace."

I bowed before him and promised that I would not disappoint him.

Back at the current palace, I was given chambers fit for a vizier, ate from the king's table itself, and was given an account with the treasurer that seemed ludicrously generous. I could have built a palace three times over for the sum I was given.

I slept in comfort that night, but I did not sleep well. Instead, I tossed and turned and wondered how in the name of heaven I was going to escape from my new employment with my head intact.

✳✳✳   ✳✳✳   ✳✳✳

The next day the King left to see to his interests abroad, and I got acquainted with my new home. I set up my household and adjusted to the discomfort of being waited upon. I also adjusted to the weight of coin in my pocket, more than I have ever seen in one place before. But what I found most challenging was going out among the people themselves.

Now, we have poverty in Israel, but never in my life have I seen such destitution. It cut at my heart to see it—the beggars lined up along the temple wall. So many people stricken with leprosy, missing limbs and eyes. So much illness. So much death. So much *need*.

A woman threw herself at my feet, cradling a skeletal infant. She raised her hand, hoping against hope I might give her a coin.

I knew how rich men responded to such entreaties. It was how they stayed rich.

I looked around for help, and suddenly there was a man at my shoulder. I didn't recognize him, but his voice was warm and familiar. "You are a carpenter," he said.

"Hello, brother," I answered, so relieved it didn't occur to me to be angry.

"You are employed to build a palace," he said.

"Yes," I said. "It is an impossibly large task."

"It will be a beautiful palace," he said. "But you must begin by purchasing stones."

The man looked at the woman. I looked up at him in confusion. Then I understood. I reached into my purse and pulled forth a rupee and placed it in her palm. She shrieked with joy, and then wept, rocking at my feet and bathing them in her tears.

"This will be a palace built of living stones,"[47] the man said. And then he stepped away and was lost in the crowd.

And so I spent the next year traveling to the farthest reaches of India, from North to South and from East to West. All along the way I purchased living stones. As I traveled, India became a palace worthy of any King.

*** *** ***

By the time Gundaphorus returned, I had exhausted my budget...and then some. I had also dispensed the whole of my wages, and I had sold my furnishings and new clothing besides—anything to purchase another stone.

When the King summoned me, I was wearing the same homespun tunic I had worn at sea on my journey here. As I knelt before the King, I felt his dark eyes glowering at me.

"Have you built me a palace?" he asked.

"I have," I answered him.

"Then let us go to see it," he said, his voice full of venom. Obviously, someone had informed him of my activities.

"That might be difficult," I said, filled with a strange boldness that I did not understand. "Your palace is in a different Kingdom. To behold it, you must learn to see in a different way."

This did not please him. So I added, "Or you could simply wait. When you depart this life, then you will see it as clear as day."

I kept my eyes lowered, but I tried to smile reassuringly. He was *not* reassured. Instead, he had me bound in chains. And *that* was when I first visited *this* fine establishment. Fond memories....[48]

Rumor had it that I was sentenced to die in the morning. But then something extraordinary happened, because in the morning I was summoned to the Palace again. I went in all my finery—by which I mean my chains—and feeling strangely light of heart, I knelt before him.

Yet this time he did not seem angry. He looked shaken. Instead of sitting high above me on his throne, he had a chair set down so close to me that I could have touched him if I had dared.

I remained kneeling, of course, but I dared to look him full in the face. And he looked terrible, like a man who had not slept. And when he spoke his voice was thin and tired.

"My brother Gad...died last night."

I wanted to touch his arm, to comfort him. But I restrained myself. "I am so terribly sorry," I said to him. "How can I help?"

"I put you in prison, and you want to help?" he asked me.

"Of course," I said. "I don't want to see anyone suffer. Not a dog, not your subjects, and certainly not you—"

He held up his hand—I was silent. He collected himself and continued. "He died suddenly. I didn't even have time to say goodbye. I visited his body, and it was cold."

I knew something of cold brothers presumed dead, but I kept my mouth shut. I nodded for him to continue.

"I kissed him and told the servants to prepare him for the burning ghats in the morning. But while they were preparing his body, he suddenly sat upright and began speaking to them."

Now, this too, I have some experience with. "What happened then?" I asked.

"He called for me, and so of course, I rushed to him. I could scarcely believe it. He had been dead, I had seen it! And yet here he was, risen, and speaking!"

"Can see how that might be…unsettling," I said with an encouraging smile.

"My brother said, 'I believe that if any asked for half your kingdom for my sake, you would give it to them.' I told him that this was indeed true. 'Then grant me one favor, brother, whatever I ask?' 'It is as good as done,' I assured him, so grateful to have my brother returned to me from the grave!

"'Swear it to me!' he said. 'I swear!' I told him. 'Tell me what I can do for you!'

"Then his eyes took on a faraway look, remembering. 'I was dead,' he said, and the devas bore me to the abode of Vishnu. And I saw palace after palace, and I began to wonder, will one of these be my dwelling place? And then I saw the most magnificent palace I have ever beheld—it was glorious, beautiful, and it shimmered in the light as if the stones themselves were alive!

"And so I asked the devas, 'Could it be that this most beautiful palace could be my home?' But they said, 'No, this is not for you, for this palace belongs to your brother the King. It was built for him by Judas Thomas, the carpenter from Israel.'

"'And I pleaded with them to allow me to return so that I could speak to you. And they, in the great mercy of Vishnu, their master, brought me back.'

"He clutched at my robes and begged me, 'Sell me your palace, brother. For I cannot abide the thought of dwelling anywhere else.'" Then the King wept.

At this point I rose up and embraced him. It was a stupid thing to do, but I wasn't thinking. I was simply…moved. When his shoulders stopped shaking, I asked him, "How did you answer your brother?"

The King wiped at his eyes and said, "I told him, 'I cannot sell you that palace, but together we can go to the Hebrew and ask him to build another.'"

Then the King's brother entered—he had been listening from the door. I embraced him as well. Together, we spent years walking the whole of the land that Gundaphorus ruled. I believe the King saw his people for the first time. And all along the way, we bought living stones.[49]

***   ***   ***

Alas, King Gundaphorus was old, and the journeying was hard on him. Eventually he withdrew to his palace—his earthly palace, that is. And not long after, he moved to his heavenly one.

But I kept doing what I was doing. The good King was generous, and we built many palaces in his time, and after his time as well.

In spite of the good I was able to do in India, I confess that I was still angry at my brother. I mean, wouldn't you be? You don't forgive being sold into slavery easily. It isn't a trifle. You don't just shrug something like that away. But if I was honest, I knew that my life did not belong to me, it was not my own. It belonged to Jesus, and he was free to do with it as he chose.

It took a long time for me to see the wisdom in his betrayal. I mean, why India? Why not Gaul or Persia? But India *is* special. The Kingdom that Jesus showed me was…heresy in Judea. But the Kingdom here was…just the way people already believed the world to be.

I mean, if I were to say, "We are all God" in Judea, I'd be stoned to death. If I say that here, people will say, "This is common knowledge. Tell us something new." Whether they are Hindus who cite the authority of Vyasa, or Buddhists who cite the authority of Gautama, the notion that all that is is one thing is not bold to them, it is not scandalous. Wherever I went I found people who were already living in the Kingdom.

My brother was not cruel to send me here. I see that now. He was wise. For this is the one place where I might preach as he preached and not be crucified as he was.

For the whole of our lives we looked exactly alike, he and I, and yet we were so different. But over the past several years, I have grown more and more like him. I preach like he does, now. I see the world as he does. I work miracles as he does. I believe I have even grown closer to his own inscrutable temperament, although I am not sure this is an improvement.

But you grow to be like the people you spend time with, you know. And although he was seen only by me, we spent a lot of time together as we roamed India.

I realized just how like him I had become when I came across a group of villagers gathered around the body of a young man. He had been bitten by a naga—a snake—who had then slithered off into its hole.

I put my hand on the man's neck, but there was no pulse. I admit it now, it made me angry. I had no right to be angry at the naga, this is what nagas *do*, after all. But it pained my heart to see such a young man struck down before his time.

So taking my walking stick, I marched over to the naga's hole and pounded the ground. "Come out, foul beast!" I bellowed. "Come out and face your judgment!"

To be honest, I had no idea what I meant by that. But I was feeling plenty judgmental toward the beast. In a few moments, a long black serpent slid out of the hole and faced me.

He reared up, spread the hood on his neck, and seemed to make a short bow. A bit surprised, I bowed in return. My mother taught me well.

"Tell me, naga, why have you bitten this young man? Answer me, or it will not go well for you."

The snake bobbed its hooded head and hissed, "I think if I *do* answer you, it will not go well for me."

I ignored his prophecy. "And yet, I compel you to answer me. Why have you stolen this man's life from him?"

"There is a woman I love," the snake hissed. "And I saw this man kissing her. And *more* than kissing…" The serpent uncoiled his body as if shuddering in revulsion at what he had seen. "A madness came upon me, and I bit him. If I could not have her… neither would he."

"Have you not heard from your own teachers," I scolded him, "that desire is the cause of all evil? To covet what your neighbor has is a sin against God."

"So Gautama has said to us," the serpent hissed in agreement, lowering his head. "And the nagas are a friend to Gautama."

Suddenly Jesus was at my elbow. "Remember James?" he whispered to me. "When that snake bit him?"

I laughed and whispered back, "Yes. I was terribly envious of you. I remember wishing at the time that I could save someone from a snakebite."

Jesus clapped me on the shoulder. "Now's your chance, little brother. But be dramatic. Might as well give these folks something to talk about." And then he was gone.

I rose to my full height, and said in a commanding tone, "You must atone for the evil you have done, naga. You must bite this young man again—but this time you must suck *out* your poison. And you must do it now, with all of us as witnesses!"

The villagers gathered breathlessly around me, all eyes intent upon the naga. Hesitantly, the naga slithered toward the young man, and once again fixed his fangs on the youth's arm. The naga began to swell up, and gradually color returned to the young man's face.

I knelt by him, and touched his face. "In the name of the one who is able to read the present moment,[50] Jesus my brother, I tell you to rise up and return to your life."

And then the young man's eyelids flickered, and he opened his eyes. Then he sat up and looked around him, as if seeing everything for the first time. But then he looked at me, and he seemed fearful. I put a reassuring hand on his arm.

"Don't be troubled, my boy," I said.

"But…there are two of you," he said. "And wherever I look, one of you is there. And one of you told the other of you to raise me up."

"When you are in between the worlds, you can see all things," I nodded. "There is nothing hidden that will not be revealed. But be at peace. There are not two of me, but only me and my brother, who looks very much like me. But he, it is true, is everywhere. Come with me, and I will teach you to be the same."

I lifted him to his feet, and his friends and family rushed up to support him.

I remembered how I felt all those years ago, when Jesus had saved our younger brother James. I wished I could do something like that. I didn't understand at the time that it wasn't Jesus doing it, but God who is All-in-all.

But as I watched that young man limping home, I understood it perfectly. I did not raise that man, God did. It was my place simply to point to that power that is both within us and beyond us. I wanted to be like Jesus, in more than just the similarity of our faces. And what do you know? I am.[51]

*** *** ***

Apparently, the young man had had enough excitement and decided not to come with me. So, alone, I made my way back to Malabar. As I got closer to the city, I felt a festivity in the air that was infectious.

I joined a band of villagers walking together and asked them where they were going. "Today is the wedding of the King's daughter, Asha," they told me. "Everyone is invited, and there will be feasting for all!"

Now, my belly rumbles with the best of them, and the idea of offering my blessing to the union delighted me—if the Brahmins would allow it, of course.

I left a message for the king with one of the guards, and took my place on a cushion on the ground in one of the outer court-yards. Musicians were playing, and there was much boasting and laughter and wine.

After a while, a servant girl passed by with a jar of wine. I found her fascinating, because she looked like she could have stepped right out of a village near Nazareth.

After so many years among the Indians, it made my heart leap to see someone from my own country. As she poured for me I said, in Aramaic, "Thank you," and to my great astonishment, she replied in Aramaic as well.

I wondered what *her* story was, and what had brought her all the way to the land of the Indians? Had, she, too, been sold as a slave? It was all too likely.

Not everyone was as hospitable as the wine-bearer. A young man taking advantage of the King's generosity was selling cups. Now, I hadn't had opportunity to clean up from the road. He apparently noticed my clothes, decided I was a beggar and gave my ear a cuff as he walked by. It wasn't a light cuff, either, and I found myself rolling on the ground in pain.

I called out a curse: "May the hand that struck me be dragged by dogs!" I thought it was a pretty good curse at the time, but of course I shouted it in Aramaic, so he never knew what I said.

But then, about a half an hour later, this dog ran by me carrying a severed arm in its teeth! It was a distressing sight, but not half so distressing as when the young Jewish wine pourer reappeared, leading several soldiers.

She pointed at me, and said, "He's the one. He cursed that boy. He said that his limbs would be dragged off by dogs."

"Is this true?" the guard asked. "Did you declare that this boy's hand would be dragged by dogs?"

"I did," I confessed. "But I didn't mean any real harm by it."

"Your curse has come true," the guard said, and his eyes were wide. "You must come with us."

"I will come," I said, "but only tell me what has happened."

The Jewish girl spoke, keeping her eyes on the ground in deference. "After you cursed that man, he went to a well to draw water and was attacked by a tiger."[52]

"That's terrible," I said, horrified at what my careless words had brought about.

I remembered Jesus cursing Levi when we were children. I *had* become like him—cursing this boy, raising the young man bitten by the naga. It was deeply unsettling, but I was given no time to ponder it, because the soldiers starting prodding me roughly.

They marched me to an enormous, scarlet pavilion. The soldiers led us through the drapes that served as doors to the pavilion, and there before me was King Misdaeus, the son of Gundaphorus. The last time I had seen him, he was just a boy. Now he was seeing his own daughter married.

He spoke a sharp word of dismissal and the guards left us. "Sadhu," he said, greeting me.

I bowed. "Congratulations, your majesty," I said. "This is a day of great joy."

"Not for the boy mangled by tigers," he said.

It was hard to argue with that, so I held my tongue.

"Promise me you will refrain from cursing any more of my servants this day. You have the ear of the gods like no other man in India."

"I promise," I said.

"And since the gods listen to you," he said, "you will lay hands on my daughter and her new husband, and pray for their happiness and prosperity."

I bowed again. "It would be my great pleasure, your majesty."

My smile was genuine. I love to pray! And to pray for someone's good rather than their destruction seemed more than fair following the day's unpleasantness thus far.

So I met the young couple and blessed them, and sent them off to their bridal chamber. Then I headed off to hire a bath and a bed.

The sun was barely peeking over the horizon when I awoke to pounding on my door. Before I could even get to my feet, I heard a crash, and soldiers burst into my room.

Without even allowing me to dress properly, they pushed me roughly out onto the street and marched me to the palace, where I was thrown into a heap at the feet of the king.

"What do you have to say for yourself, Hebrew?" he asked. His voice was as bitter as bile.

"My lord," I said, "in your own sight I gave my blessing to your daughter and her husband. Then I went to bed. I know of nothing else."

"How many years you have been employed by this Kingdom, and yet you lie to me? You are called a holy man throughout this kingdom, and yet you lie to me?"

"I tell you the simple truth. Please, your majesty," I said, keeping my gaze low, "tell me what happened. Perhaps together we can reason it out."

"You know full well what happened," the King spat. "We left the royal couple in their bridal chamber. It was their *wedding night*."

"I understand, your majesty," I said. "But humor me. Assume I do not know, and tell me what happened then. Please."

"When a maid went to check on the couple in the tender hours of the morning, she found *you* sitting with them on the bed. They were still dressed in their clothes from last night! There was no stain on the sheet! Instead, my daughter was talking excitedly about her 'true' husband, a man who has never set foot in this country, with the ridiculous name of *Jee-zuss*."

I wanted to point out that it was not, strictly speaking, true that Jesus had never set foot on Indian soil, but it seemed wise to keep my head low.

"We trusted you, Hebrew. My father gave you your freedom, he was your patron, and in return you have convinced my daughter and her husband to live as brother and sister for the rest of their lives, never to consummate their marriage! Never to give us an heir!

"You had the nerve to tell them that the flesh was corrupt, and the life that such a carnal union would bring forth would be corrupt and temporary. You told them that only a spiritual union would bring forth eternal life. And now they both claim to be married to some Judean king, which makes no sense at all for a whole host of reasons. Why have you betrayed us?"

I felt a sinking feeling in my gut. "This man your servant saw talking with your daughter—he looked exactly like me?" I asked.

"She swore to me on her knees that it was you and you alone!" the King shouted, his face blazing red.

"Did she call a guard?" I asked.

"She did," the King replied.

"And when that guard seized him, was he…cold?"

The King cocked his head, wondering where my question could possibly lead. "When the guard arrived, you were *gone*."

"And did anyone see me…him…go?" I asked.

"No." The King looked momentarily troubled. "You seemed to simply disappear."

"I was afraid of that," I said.

"Do you dare to deny that you were in that Bridal chamber?" he thundered.

"I do deny it," I said. "It must have been my twin brother."

"Do you mock me, Hebrew?" the King's eyes narrowed.

"I do not, your majesty. I am a twin—it is what my nickname means! And my brother Jesus looks *exactly* like me."

"And is he in India? Why have we never seen him?"

I sighed, not knowing how to explain this. "He is everywhere, your majesty."

"You *do* mock me," he said. "And for that, you will die."

*** *** ***

And that is how I have ended up back here, sharing these luxurious accommodations with you.

Forgive me if I keep watching the window. I have always loved daybreak—it is my favorite time of day. It seems cruel that on *this* day, it should herald my death.

I keep running through the King's words in my mind. Why would Jesus do this? Yet, it is the story of our entire lives together. Just when I think I have him figured out, he slips sideways and utterly confounds me. I fear I will *never* understand him.

Why did he tell that couple that their knowledge of one another would make them unclean? He always encouraged people in their passions—he got into trouble himself over that very thing—he loved wine, he loved parties,[53] he let low women rub his feet.

I know he doesn't believe what he told that couple—so why did he say it? Why would he intentionally mislead them? Why would he place me in a situation where he knew I would be blamed for it?

I cannot puzzle it out. I thought I knew him—clearly I don't. I thought he had outgrown his childish mischief—but now...I don't know.

I thought we saw with one eye—clearly that is not true. Either he cares nothing for me, or...he must see something that I do not see.

I must cling to that, because I cannot bear the other. I love my brother...but I confess to you that I do not trust him. And I so dearly *want* to trust him. But how can I? It makes no logical *sense* to trust him. Not now.

I have sought. I have found. And I have been deeply troubled. When will I rule, Jesus?[54]

There is no trust bubbling up within me for him. If I am to trust him, I must wrestle it from my bowels by force of will alone. I must *choose* to trust him.

I know this: I saw him raise Zeno with my own eyes. I saw

him raise James. I saw him raise Lazarus. I saw his own body, risen from the grave. I put my hands where the nails were driven in. Where the spear pierced him, I put my hand. But if I march to my death, if I do what he asks me to do—will he raise *me*?

I remember once, after he was raised, he said to me, "Do not think of resurrection as an illusion, brother. Instead, it is the world that is the illusion.[55] Resurrection is what is real."

I so dearly want to believe that. It may be the only thing I can cling to now. I must *choose* to trust him.

Did you hear that? It is the rooster. And there is the first ray of the sun. Already I can hear the soldier's boots on the road.

I must choose. Tell me, fellow prisoners, my friends, you who have heard my testimony—if you had seen what I have seen, how would you choose? Would you trust him? Could you?

End Notes

[1]   Infancy Gospel of Thomas, 4-5.

[2]   Infancy Gospel of Thomas 2:1-3:3.

[3]   Infancy Gospel of Thomas 6-7

[4]   Infancy Gospel of Thomas 13

[5]   Infancy Gospel of Thomas 9:1-2

[6]   Compare Matthew 3:13-17, Mark 1:9-11, and Luke 3:21-23.

[7]   Mark 3:21

[8]   Mark 2:31-32

[9]   Gospel of Thomas 101

[10] Gospel of Thomas 17

[11] Gospel of Thomas 7

[12] Gospel of Thomas 77

[13] The Book of Thomas the Contender

[14] This exchange is a conflation of Gospel of Thomas logia 6 and 14.

[15] Gospel of Thomas 14

[16] John 6:60

[17] Gospel of Thomas 6

[18] Gospel of Thomas 2

[19] Gospel of Thomas 108

[20] Gospel of Philip 67

21   Gospel of Thomas 5

22   Gospel of Thomas 113

23   Gospel of Thomas 3

24   Gospel of Thomas 97

25   Gospel of Thomas 113

26   Psalm 24:1

27   Gospel of Thomas 3

28   Luke 10:38-42

29   Gospel of Thomas 114

30   Gospel of Thomas 22

31   Gospel of Thomas 13

32   Gospel of Thomas 25

33   John 20

34   John 20:28

35   The Book of Thomas the Contender

36   The Book of Thomas the Contender

37   The Book of Thomas the Contender

38   The Book of Thomas the Contender

39   Gospel of Thomas 72

40   Galatians 6:7

41   The Book of Thomas the Contender

42   Gospel of Thomas 38

43   Matthew 18:20

44   Acts of Thomas I:1

45   Acts of Thomas I:2-3

46   Gospel of Thomas 82

47   1 Peter 2:5

48   Acts of Thomas III:17-21

49   Acts of Thomas II:22-26

50   Gospel of Thomas 91

51   Acts of Thomas III:31-34

52   Acts of Thomas I:5-9; the text says "lion," but lions are not native to the Malabar region of India. I have changed it to "tiger," a far more prevalent predatory feline in the region.

53   Luke 7:34

54   Gospel of Thomas 2

55   Treatise on the Resurrection

If you enjoyed this story,
please try John R. Mabry's other fiction:

What Child is This? (A Christmas at Bremmer's Novel)

When an abandoned baby is left on the loading dock at the height of the seasonal rush, the indecisive but soft-hearted manager and a madcap cast of employees scramble to care for her. As the town Sheriff copes with deep personal loss, he finds grace in solving the mystery of the baby's origin. The new Lutheran pastor—Munich's first female clergyperson—feels rejected by her parishioners, but discovers her purpose and worth as she lends her wisdom and guidance to the crisis.

Reviewers say:

"What a truly delightful heavenly story to read!"

"Heart-warming, fun, and though holiday themed, this book is a joy for any time of the year!"

"I wanted a Christmas book and this was fabulous. It was emotional, sweet and just beautiful."

If you would like to know more about the theology of the Thomas school of early Christianity, please read:

The Way of Thomas:
Nine Insights for Enlightened Living
from the Secret Sayings of Jesus

This book highlights the differences between the teachings of Thomas' Jesus and Paul's. For the Jesus of Thomas is not a savior come down from heaven, but a man who has awakened to the truth of the interconnectedness of all things. The parallels to Buddhism are numerous. It is in this lost Gospel that Christianity, Judaism, and Buddhism meet as a single, coherent message. This book consolidates these forgotten teachings into nine inspiring, easy-to-grasp insights that make this ancient book a practical guide for contemporary spiritual seekers of any—or no—tradition.

Reviewers say:

"I found that reading the book and contemplating the exercises re-engaged my own sense of the mystery of God."

"*The Way of Thomas* gives nine insights in improving one's spirituality! I really enjoyed reading the book and am using it as a textbook on being more like Jesus. This book is a *must* read!"

"Mabry's book is the leading edge of at least the next hundred years of exploration of a new look and a new way of understanding and benefitting from the life that Jesus chose to lead."

www.ingramcontent.com/pod-product-compliance
Lightning Source LLC
Chambersburg PA
CBHW020643250626
47154CB00008B/2795